C000264917

Losing You

Previous Publications

How to Be a Dragonfly (Smith Doorstop Books, 2005)

Losing You

Patricia Debney

Published by bluechrome publishing 2007

2 4 6 8 10 9 7 5 3 1

First published in Great Britain in 2007 by
bluechrome publishing
PO Box 109,
Portishead, Bristol. BS20 7ZJ

www.bluechrome.co.uk

A CIP catalogue record for this book is available from the
British Library.

ISBN 978-1-906061-06-7 hardback
ISBN 978-1-904781-47-9 paperback

Printed by Biddles Ltd, King's Lynn, Norfolk

For the loves of my life,
past and present

Acknowledgements

An extract from this novel first appeared in *New Writing 10* (Picador, 2001).

somewhere i have never travelled,gladly beyond
any experience,your eyes have their silence:
in your most frail gesture are things which enclose me,
or which i cannot touch because they are too near

E.E. Cummings

Marilyn

Tuesday

Lewis comes in to wake us up as usual – it's 7 o'clock, give or take. Doug lifts him over, groaning, "Christ," he says. Lewis settles between us, squirrelling under the covers, his thumb in his mouth.

I have just closed my eyes when I feel Lewis' hand come to rest gently on the side of my face. I open my eyes to see his straight in front of me, brown like his father's. He is at his best in the mornings, perhaps all children are: unnaturally bright-eyed, almost feverish looking, still, as contemplative as a six year old can be.

"Mom," he says now, evenly, "what happens when you die?"

Doug shifts slightly and turns his head toward me, waiting for my answer. Of course, it's not the first time Lewis has asked something like this, but he's older now, and I can see he wants something different. Which part of the story should I tell?

I say, "Your heart stops pushing blood around your body and your lungs stop working so you can't breathe. Everything just...stops." Doug grunts. I agree with him, not really satisfactory. I want to say that you disappear, but that's not true, we don't; we don't dissolve like the wicked witch when we go.

Lewis pulls his hand away and turns onto his back, in imitation of his father. "Like something's broken," he says.

"Yes."

"Like when batteries stop working."

"Yes. Something like that." I can see what the next question will be, and sure enough, it comes.

"Why can't you fix it?"

Doug sighs, turns onto his side and puts an arm over Lewis' stomach. "It's hard to understand, Lew," he says, "but that's what happens. When someone dies, they stop working forever, there's no way to fix them."

His father's voice has more finality than mine, and Lewis is temporarily satisfied. "Will I die?" he says.

"Yes," says Doug. "but not for a very long time."

"Will you die?"

"Yes. Everyone dies, Lewis, but not until they're very, very old."

"Like Grandad."

My heart pounds as Doug answers, "Yes, that's right, like Grandad."

After breakfast, I watch the two of them drive up and out for the day. It's Lewis' last day of school; he can't wait for the summer. Today they will hardly manage to do anything in class, I remember it. The heat, the feeling of imminent freedom. Even me, a goody two shoes always, misbehaved on the last day. No one cared, not even the teachers. In this country it is different, however, different for Lewis. The summer is short, there's no local pool, no gang of kids to run riot with. Not that I would let him do that – or would I? What were my parents thinking when they let me loose day after day. No one seemed afraid then, that's for sure.

I go over to the kitchen sink. Best to do the dishes now, before they weigh more and more heavily through the day. As I wash I look out the kitchen window; he's lucky, a sunny day for his last day, full of the promise of summer. I can see the birds out, still early enough in the day for them: our resident woodpecker, and one of the magpies. One for sorrow, I always think, but the second is always somewhere, up in the trees, for joy.

For me now, of course, summer isn't as much fun. I will keep working, three days a week, and will try to keep Lewis occupied at friends, swimming lessons, etc. He's past the age where pottering at home is enough, yet not old enough to do anything by himself. I'd like to work in the garden, though. Perhaps I should get him digging holes for me; he digs, I plant, that might work.

As I stand there I hear footsteps, and know immediately that it's Hilary. If she's going to stop by it's always after dropping off Aaron, and in a moment she comes into view, as ever trying to tuck her hair up into its clasp, and as ever, failing.

She comes to the door. "Hiya," she says, and pecks me on the cheek. "God, what a mess I must look. I never get a chance to get it together before rushing him off." She removes the clasp and holds it in her hands. "You look great, though," she says, as if I've said something. "I don't know how you do it."

She's always like this, full of flattery. It's one of the things I find difficult about her, although I know I shouldn't. She's a kind person, I think, just lacking in self-esteem, and, as I am privy to hearing twice a week at the moment, she and Adam are having troubles.

She glances around the kitchen. "Coffee?" I say. She pauses, but we both know the answer. I put the kettle on and finish the dishes as she clears the table of the rest, the marmalade and fruit. She even wipes up the crumbs.

We sit down, and both sigh. "Lovely," she says. "Yes," I reply, and am a little surprised to notice I mean it. We sip in silence for a moment, and her fingers again travel up to her hair.

I find myself thinking that she's not very attractive, and immediately feel guilty. Not that she doesn't have life in her – that wild hair is evidence of that – but her face is rather set. Doug would say, straight out, as he does sometimes, that it's old before its time, the furrows from her nose to corners of her lips pronounced, the surprising dullness of her skin. Her eyes are a lovely brown, but rather small, or maybe just dwarfed by her gigantic hair of the same colour. Or maybe it's just the way she is, the feel of her: nervous, a little sharp, excitable, which sets me on my guard.

Nevertheless, in an odd way she's become a good, if limited, friend these last months, since we moved to this part of town. Her son, Aaron, is a year older than Lewis, and they are close, would be closer I think if we weren't all so busy. Like Lewis, he's an only child. As I am. I remember how it used to feel to meet another only child; you didn't want to be around them because it was like they knew all your secrets. So they must get on well to be such friends. Hilary and I have coffee about twice a week; she knows by now my work days, and tends to stop by the other days. We don't talk about much, quite different from the friends I left behind years ago in the States. We have nothing in common, literally, except our sons. Yet – sitting here now I realise I am rather intrigued by her, perhaps it's a professional interest. Or perhaps we're just trying to figure each other out.

"So," I say, and watch her scrunch her hair. She smiles fleetingly. "How are you?"

"Me?!" She almost laughs. "Oh, you know. Nothing new to report." I feel my stomach tighten. She's not happy today. "Aaron is like a crazy child at the moment." Her fluttery fingers, when not occupied in her hair, seem to tremble at times, like now. "And Adam, well – I'm not sure he even notices, you know. I think – well, I think Aaron is acting up for Adam's attention, really, I think he sort of misses his dad."

"It happens," I say. I take another sip of tea. "What's he been doing?"

Hilary looks at me. "Who, Aaron? Oh, you know...speaking rudely, shouting, slamming doors. Not doing what I ask. He never used to be like this, never, not even when he was a baby. He was always such a good boy."

"Hmm." I should be charging for this, I think, then stop myself. She's a friend, for God's sake. "And where's Adam, meanwhile?"

"Good point." Hilary rolls her eyes. "Where is he, indeed." She pauses, and her voice grows quieter. "I don't know, I really don't know. Not with us, I don't think, not now." Her eyes water, but she carries on. "Never bloody mind," she says. "It's all variations on a theme, isn't it?" She shifts her cup. "Bloody psychiatrists," she says, and smiles at me. "There's something about you which just makes me start talking. I'm sorry."

I shrug. "Don't worry about it. I'm only a counsellor, by the way. Not nearly so intriguing." We both laugh.

She's right, of course. I wonder if there's something in me that clicks into listening mode, everyone a client. "Whatever the case," I add, "if you need to talk, you need to talk." Like that blasted BT ad, I think, as if talking saves everything, every misunderstanding or hurt feeling.

"I guess," she says, as if reading my mind. Then, "But I feel a bit on a treadmill with the whole thing at the moment. I'm not sure that talking doesn't just make it worse somehow, rather than better."

We sit in silence. Yes, I think, there is a great deal to be said for not talking sometimes, for just *being*. I'm surprised she feels the same, being by nature such a talker. I'm surprised, really, that we can even sit here, happily, without speaking. Perhaps there's more to her than I give her credit for.

The phone rings and we both start. "Sorry," I say, although of course it's not my fault.

It's the hospital. As I watch Hilary try not to listen, they tell me that Dad died this morning. It was, they say, very peaceful. For lack of anything else to do or say, I thank them and hang up the phone. Hilary turns toward me, puts down her cup, comes over and wraps her arms around me. I don't cry. I think stupid things, I think, I was going to see him at eleven. We were going to talk about everything. Lewis had concentrated my mind, and I was going to bring him photos, Lewis' drawings, some Doritoes. God, this morning of all mornings. Today of all days.

I raise my head, rest it on Hilary's shoulder. She moves her hand to my hair and strokes it. "There now," she says, "I'm sorry. You poor thing."

After a few minues, she leaves me to get ready to go to the hospital. She will pick up Lewis and take him over to hers; they will do something nice, she says.

I find myself in front of the bathroom mirror putting on make-up, although I can't think why. There's no rush, yet I feel an urgency to get out there, to – what? See him. And what I expect to find I don't know. He's not there anymore, I know, but deep down I think I might be able to feel him somehow. And I need to look my best, I need to be there for him, for his last moments. Even though his last moments have already officially passed.

The drive out to the hospital is, perhaps ironically, quite beautiful, year round. It's more French than anything, I think again today, the tall trees now in full leaf, lining the broad road. Today, however, the journey feels more cinematic than usual; I feel as though I am sweeping, with a kind of upper class concern, up to the doors of a stately home. It *is* a stately home, that much is correct. But for years it has been a private hospital, somewhere between an old people's home and a hospice. The gardens, nevertheless, are immaculate; I can see a gardener on a mower through the trees now. The sun must be strong and heavy on his capped head. Why do we do jobs in certain ways at certain times? Why didn't he do this earlier, when it was cooler, not so hostile? I realise even as I think this that I'm avoiding the issue.

I swing up to the front car park, feeling myself to be justifiably part of an emergency. Although in a sense the emergency is over. I get out of the car, and stand and look at the silent entrance. It's something which has always unnerved me in my short association with the place, the silence surrounding it. Like no one ever makes a fuss, because they're all going to die anyway. My father, of course, didn't belong here. An American with secondaries, not someone they were wildly keen on having. There are, they hastened to tell me, plenty of people from this country who need the facilities. But as I didn't see anyone actually knocking down the doors to get in, and as my father had arrived here only weeks before with good money in his pocket and an indeterminate time to live, I insisted. Which is not something I do often, or that comes naturally. He himself was never clear about what he wanted, what he expected from his only child, given that my mother, his wife, was long since dead. He'd arrived, it seems, almost on a whim, only phoning me the week before. I went to meet him, of course, and knew immediately something was wrong: he was full of bluster as usual, tanned, and recounted golf stories almost from the minute we got in the car. But suddenly he'd had to stop, draw breath. He'd rested his head on the seat and closed his eyes.

What was he thinking, coming to a strange country to die? But then, put like that, what are any of us doing, me and Doug included, going anywhere? "If you're going to go, you might as well make it far away." This is my mother speaking, the great traveller. From the old school of British women, inheritors of the Victorian travellers. Her story is to some extent the usual one: married an American in the war and her parents never forgave her. She and my dad moved back to the States, settling in Ohio. Some time later I was born, a gift, she would say later, which I always took to mean a fluke. They could never have another child, much to my mother's particular deep regret.

Now, as at several times when I have felt alone here in Britain, I remember that my mother's brother and sister are probably still alive. Living somewhere in Lancashire I think. When I was twelve we came over to see the family, just after my mother's mother died – of a sudden stroke, same as my mother. The whole thing, all those years ago, was a ghastly experience. Britain and America were much more differentiated then than they are now. I spoke painfully differently from the other children. The food turned my stomach. My mother cried all the time, not making a sound, sitting in the undersized chair in her room. My father rumbled around in his way, full of false cheer. When we got back home, my mother seemed to sleep for days. My father guided me around the house, around her, feeding me, taking me swimming. Jet lag, he said, but of course it wasn't true. None of us, to my knowledge, have seen her family since.

It seems unimaginable in some way that my father should have died here, in a country my mother came almost to despise. Then again, she never even knew that Doug and I had moved here, my father keeping it from her for a while, keeping it from her as it turned out, until she died. So coming here, I guess, was only a little bit more of what had come before.

And now he's dead, the bugger, right here, only a few feet away. I can't go in, and take two steps back to lean on the car. The feeling that I've had all my life, which has floated around the outside for as long as I can remember, is finally true. And that is, that I am all alone. That really, nothing, and no one, matters. I am just standing here at the stern of a boat, and the wind is almost pushing me over. I hold on to something behind me, just to stay upright. And I cannot take my eyes off of the line of black clouds just above the yellow horizon.

Some minutes later, having made it to the nurse's station, I'm trying to get up the nerve to go in and see him. They've given me a cup of coffee. Of course people must die here all the time, I think. Maybe if I can get a look into another room I'll know what to expect: covered or uncovered, curtains open or drawn.

I look up. There is a man standing next to me, leaning over the counter and pointing at something in a file. He straightens up, turns slightly toward me. He looks familiar, or at least as if I should know who he is. One of my father's doctors perhaps.

He glances up at me, more to move around me than anything, then stops. "It's Marilyn, isn't it?" Then, seeing that I don't recognise him, he holds out his hand to shake. "Adam, Aaron's dad. Hilary's husband," he adds.

I shake his hand. "Oh right," I say.

"We met at the school once," he goes on, "I was waiting in the car." He pauses. "No?" He gives a little laugh. "Oh well. You obviously made more of an impression on me than I did on you."

In the meantime I've noticed he has a name tag on, an official one. He follows my eyes. "Just popping in," he explains, "to see one of my patients."

I remember now Hilary's complaints about the surgery – Adam's time commitments, his anxiety. Only I must admit that now he looks relaxed, even a little concerned for me.

"And you?" he says. He touches my elbow lightly, briefly. "What brings you to this lovely place?"

For the first time since hearing the news, I start crying. He puts his hand over my hand, which I withdraw to reach for a tissue. "It's my father, he died here this morning."

The nurse, who's been hovering close, clears my cup. She even takes a cloth and wipes the space where the cup had been. Adam and I step away, and he turns more fully toward me.

"I'm sorry," he says. "Can I do anything?"

I shake my head. The tears are flowing freely now and I hold the tissue up to my nose, can't talk. I cry badly, messily, and even now I'm paranoid about how my nose always drips. I close my eyes and feel myself sway slightly. I could go to sleep, I really could. I can feel something lying in wait for me, something I haven't even started to think about yet. I have no idea what it is. But if I can just sleep, maybe it will pass off, recede into the safe distance.

Adam guides me to a chair. I sense him looking around, and as luck would have it I hear Doug's careful footsteps coming down the hallway. He hates hospitals, usually feels ill just being in them, but he's here. He stops, probably confused by the presence of Adam. I open my eyes and look at the floor, the shiny variegated lino tiles. Thankfully, they introduce themselves. God knows what Doug thinks but right now I don't care. Adam rests his hand on my shoulder – consoling, professional – and I hear him walk away.

Adam's hand is replaced by Doug's, who rubs his thumb slowly back and forth across my shoulder – a characteristic movement, one that has irritated me in the past, but that now I find unexpectedly comforting, and I reach up and touch his fingers. In all our years together, nine alone, six with Lewis, I have never doubted him. Not once. I may have been a mess, but Doug is a rock, never shakeable, always knowing what he wants and who he cares for.

He takes my hand. "Have you been in yet?" he says. I shake my head.

"Right. I think we should go. Let's get it over with. Then maybe go have a late lunch." He squeezes my hand.

"There must be a some people to ring," I say. I feel very vague. He pulls me up a little. "Come on, don't worry. All in good time."

It's something my father would say, stolen from the wicked witch convincing herself that she will get Dorothy, and the ruby slippers. Thinking about it now, I don't know why he would ever say it, a threat rather than a promise. We walk in silence down the hallway to his room.

I've never seen a dead body, not even my mother's. She died at home and I had always thought that would be best, but this isn't actually unpleasant. It's not frightening at all, really; there is an unexpected familiarity to the whole scene. Of course, I realise as I approach, he is my father, one of the only bodies I have known in my life, so it's no wonder – no wonder I want to stay with him.

I go over and sit down, take his hand. This is a shock: it does feel different, cool. But the shape is the shape I know, and I hold it.

The curtains are drawn – a gold light shines through and around them. It is warm, half dark.

I stare at him. I know he is dead. But what seems all wrong is something that seems divided from that fact, and that is, that his chest and stomach are still. There is not even the slightest rise and fall; I hold my own breath to see if I have missed something almost imperceptible, but of course nothing happens. The stillness is the most unnatural thing, and yet the most natural. I have a strong desire to join him – where? – to be with him. I don't know if it's for his sake or for mine.

Doug walks up behind me. He whispers, "You okay?"

I nod, and fight a crazy urge to laugh. Good grief, why whisper when we can't even be heard?

I stand up. Do I belong here or don't I? I look down at my father, even more jaundiced-looking with the yellow light from the curtains. I'd like to go with him, wherever he is, but part of that desire is some feeling that I need to understand something. Him, my mother, my own place? God, I don't know. He's dead.

I turn to Doug. His eyes are full of tears. "There's so much to do," I say. He nods, and we leave the room.

I can't tell Lewis that night but Doug does. I can hear them in the next room, detect Lewis' accepting silences. Then the Lego is dumped out, and I know it's over.

I move through to the dining room to begin to set out our dinner plates and glasses. Doug hears me and appears at the door. "Don't do that," he says. "Let's just get a take-out."

"I have to do something," I say. "Anyway, we went out for lunch." I look up at him, and put a plate down right where I'm holding it, in the middle of the table. "I just keep feeling that

I ought to be doing something else, that there's something else I should be doing, something I've lost track of." I sit down. "It's like when Lewis was born. I kept feeling that whenever I didn't think about him, whenever I wasn't aware of his every movement, he would disappear somehow. Like if I don't think about him, he no longer exists." Doug doesn't say anything. "I can't explain it – but there's that same feeling, like if I stop concentrating, on what I don't even know, then anything might happen... I'm sorry, I don't know what I'm saying."

"It doesn't matter," Doug says. He comes over and sits in the chair next to me. "A control freak, I think, doctor." He smiles a little, and I manage a little one back. He's right, of course, as ever.

I glance at the doorway. "So how'd he take it?"

"Oh," Doug stretches back, his arms up over his head, "you know kids. They never cease to amaze me. It was like he knew already –"

"After that stuff this morning."

"Yes. Odd."

"Mmm." What I don't mention is that none of this really surprises me. Lewis has always been a perceptive child, slightly ethereal. A Pisces. Takes after my father's mother, who, the rare times I spoke to her or saw her, seemed to conduct her life almost exclusively according to 'feelings'. "I had a feeling you would call," she would say. Or, "I thought you might come soon." Her eyes, too, similar to Lewis', similar in fact to mine, although I've never been convinced about my own powers – whether I have any at all, that is.

I can hear him now, padding through with some Lego creation. "Dad, look!"

Doug turns to him. "Well done, son. Now – it's almost bedtime. Let's finish this off then go up." As he stands, Doug reaches out and squeezes my hand. "You stay here," he says quietly.

I am not certain I really want to be alone, but I find that I stay, lean back and close my eyes. What an awful day. I have the unfamiliar desire to talk to someone about it, briefly wonder if this is how my clients feel when they come to me, suffering from an overwhelming urge to recount, explain to the self what the self must already know. Supposedly. But there's no one, of course, to talk to, to talk to about Dad especially, with Mom gone too. No one who lived with him like I did, no one else in the world.

The old feeling I thought gone, of wishing desperately for a sibling, comes over me again. Really it's wishing for company of course, and for a world where no matter what, we would be close, comfort each other, understand each other. Be there for each other. But how many families have that relationship? You can pick friends, as they say, but not family. So – no harm done.

And yet – my mind swings to Lewis – harm *is* done. Or might be. As I sit here, I feel I am doing him harm by keeping him alone, denying him another dimension to his life. It's a regret only sometimes, I think, but it is a regret, much like my mother's I suppose. Except Doug and I chose this, we decided what was best for us.

I can't help a sigh. So we have denied ourselves as well, like too much of a good thing might be bad. How Protestant. But now, no matter what I might want from time to time, now it's most definitely too late. It has to be the end of the story; we've discussed it many times.

Enough. I pull the chair over to the long window which looks out to the street. It is drizzling a little; I can see the reflection of the grey sky on the roads. A man walks by holding a newspaper under his jacket, a teenager sprints past, late for dinner perhaps. Upstairs, I hear Lewis thunder from the bathroom to the bedroom, laughing his head off.

In so far as I ever get homesick, this time of day does it. In Ohio a profound silence settles about this time, or perhaps it's just that any sound seems to stop as soon as it starts – you can barely hear, say, the dull hit of a bat on a ball, the muted cries of the children running between the bases. I suppose it was a time when no one pretended to be doing anything, to be busier or any more interesting than they were. I would look out then, sitting on the front porch, even as a child, and stare at the mostly empty streets, hear my mother and father behind me, in the house, saying grown up things about work and neighbours. I know by now that I was deeply lonely as a child, and by the age of six or seven – Lewis' age – I had already developed an elaborate world of my own which I preferred to adult company. And the quiet of this time of day was part of it – uninterrupted, when anything could happen, when I could go on some long journey and take a long time to get home, or come back somehow changed.

Now, as I look out of the window, I long for those times, or something like them, for a liberating kind of aloneness, and feel instead a loneliness that has built into it – I can feel it now – a kind of emptiness. Made worse, of course, by today. The constant, not always unpleasant, cul-de-sac of grown up life.

It has become dusk as I sit here, and I wonder for how long someone has been standing by the gate at the end of path. In the growing dark now I can see the person move, coming toward the house, and I instinctively duck out of view, behind the curtains.

The doorbell does not ring, however, and after a minute I look out. I just catch the retreating figure of a woman – she turns toward the street lamp, now finally flickering on. It's Hilary, and my heart does something I don't recognise. I wonder if she has seen me hiding.

Why did she come? I go to the front door, open it and look out. There, on the doorstep, is a bunch of flowers and a card. Rather macabre, I think, the habit of this country, always leaving flowers where someone has died. I am not sure whether they are for me or my father; nevertheless I take them inside, arrange them and set them on the dining room table, where they will be out of direct sunlight.

They are heavy summer flowers, tiger lilies, and even with all the windows open, that night lying in bed I can smell their perfume, a breeze blowing it through the house.

Of course, I can't sleep, I've never been able to sleep in the heat. Every minute or so a car goes by outside, like the steady rush of waves against the shore. This should put me to sleep, but instead it seems to hypnotise me. I imagine the waxy lilies downstairs slowly opening, their spotted petals bending further and further back. I remember the pungent centre of each flower, stamens loaded with rusty pollen that stains if you're not careful.

I remember my mother's funeral, the whole house full of flowers by the time I arrived, my poor father drowning in them. People mean well, they always do, but my mother was simple, with simple tastes – a few flowers and leaves from the garden, a particularly nice rose. Nothing fancy. And I will never forget my father's inability in the face of it – the bouquets were nearly all white, as I remember, arranged into tight, easy to keep bunches, stuffed into that green foam. He'd just put them down any old place, any old how, and when I got there every surface, the kitchen table included, was covered. Since then I've never sent flowers to anyone, probably, I think now, because I'm just not brave enough to send bright colours. Hilary, on the other hand: I can smell the lilies again, rich and quite mysterious. I do her a disservice, perhaps – at least they aren't carnations. At least they have a sort of rude life to them, and, in their own way, are beautiful.

Doug breathes quietly next to me. I can sense that he is on the verge of waking-up himself – we have done this our whole lives together, our clocks ticking virtually in unison. Sometimes I even pretend that I am not awake, because I know that soon he too will wake up, and then we will both be tired in the morning for no good reason.

Now he stirs, and I breathe as if I'm sleeping. If I close my eyes, I can almost believe that I am sleeping, dozing just a little, enough to keep the night from being truly interrupted. Like a baby, he needs to be settled off to sleep. The thought creeps into my mind – all the more reason not to have another one. But I push it away. It's been a hard day.

At a lull in the traffic I find myself drifting off for real. In the mess in my head I see my father lying dead in the hospital room, his strong face in profile. Something smells perfume-y. I think it's him, but I know it's not, it's a woman's smell. In a funny sort of way it seems to be all over me, and I'm wondering if I smell – smell like a woman, that is, *that* smell that needs hiding.

My father is lying dead, a look of utter blankness on his face, impossible to disturb him. Yet I begin to feel that mounting panic which tells my conscious mind that I am dreaming now and that I must get out. There is the pervading smell of sex, sexiness, and I begin to back out of the room, arms out, trying to take the smell out with me. I want to get it away from him, but I am also hoping it will leave me.

Good Lord. I jerk awake and break into a cold sweat as soon as I open my eyes. The skin on my neck is prickling. Come in Freud, I think. Incredible that a counsellor can mix up sex and death. But I have. And knowing it doesn't make anything any clearer. And my father has died, the one who always made me smile. There. Grief comes over me, and I pull it up, like a blanket, under my chin for comfort.

Friday

Of course, the day of Dad's funeral would be full of brightness. Odd that, like the day he died, the full sun. Rain in between.

I am up early. Doug does Lewis, and I field the tiny things that seem insurmountable: a representative from the home stops by with some flowers and a note saying they've given £20 to cancer research. Right, I think, so that's where Dad's money has gone.

The flowers are white carnations. No pink or red, of course. Too close to something, to sickness, or blood. Like getting married, the red stain saved for after the wedding night, the sheets hung out for all to see. What is it about white?

I look up at the mantelpiece. I did actually get married in white – ivory – I don't know why, and there's the picture to prove it. We'd been living together so long by then it now seems quite ridiculous. But we will engage in rituals, go through the motions of the way we think things should be, however absurd. And who ever gets it right? The invisible *it*. Meanwhile, we keep someone happy by trying too hard.

Like this wake. I've engaged with ritual to such an extent that I've even made the sausage rolls for it. *Made* them, as if it mattered.

As I stare at the sausage rolls I notice how close in colour they are to the crisps, and indeed to the corresponding brown glinting on the tops of the quiches, homemade again. Even the skins of the new potatoes. All lined up for consumption as if it's a reasonable thing to do, go through this. The appearance of everyday, the comforts of home.

Through the monitor I can hear Doug trying to reason with Lewis, get him into his new smart clothes. Especially for weddings and funerals. I feel slightly sick.

I go to the breakfast table and sit down. Christ, Christ, Christ. Hilary will be here soon and I am in this useless state.

I stand up again. Yes, I hear her steps down the drive. I go to the door and open it.

"Hi." She leans toward me, rests one hand on my upper arm. Her hair is tamed back, and it suits her. She has on a navy blue and white suit and is wearing almost maroon lipstick. She kisses me on the cheek, an air kiss to save her lips and my skin –

but her cheek against mine is soft. She squeezes my arm as she pulls back. "How are you?"

"Well…" I meet her eyes, which are full, as far as I can see, of a genuine concern. "How am I not, is probably more like it."

"Oh dear." She moves away, and reaches in to the carrier bag she is holding. She unloads a carrot cake in a tupperware container onto the counter. She turns back to me, waiting.

"I'm not feeling anything," I say. "I'm not able to think of what to wear, I can't think of what to say to Doug or Lewis." I take a step toward the kitchen window and look out of it, to the sun belting down. "And I miss my mother very much." I know but don't tell her the reasons for this: wanting someone who really knew my father, wanting to talk about him. Wanting someone, anyone, to have long memories of him, way back to when he was in his prime. But no one coming today except Doug and Lewis will have even met him, and I can't help feeling that he's died alone.

She comes and stands next to me, looking out too. I am crying again, of course. Her arm slips around my waist, her hand resting on my hip. I can feel the heat of it through my summer dressing gown. I am surprised how much this move unnerves me; it used to be quite usual between all us girls in college, physical affection. But now – my reaction just reminds me of how far I am away from myself, something I've been thinking about recently, and not just because of Dad. I've ended-up, it seems, being not quite who I thought I was.

I force myself to turn to her and give her a hug. She pulls me close, and I can feel her breasts squeeze against mine, the underwire of her bra. She wraps both arms around me, and I find myself resting my head for a moment on her shoulder. There's something very different about holding a woman, I think. Whatever sexuality is there seems to follow whole different paths, whole different ways of getting somewhere. Like a circuit, throwing a switch, the electricity tracing through little used wires.

We are just pulling apart as Doug and Lewis come in, all dressed.

"Hello Hilary." Doug holds out a hand. "Nice to see you." He spots the carrot cake. "Thanks for dropping by. It's all a bit..." He trails off. I know he was about to say "of a mess," but I can't bring myself to care too much. He's right.

Hilary picks up the signals. "It's a difficult time, of course," she says, "I'm just glad we're around." She looks at

Lewis, quiet in his new trousers and blue shirt. "Hiya, darling," she says, "don't you look smart?"

Lewis stands halfway behind Doug. "Grandad's funeral today," he says.

"Yes." Hilary squats down to him. "And I know you're going to be a good boy." She ruffles his hair.

"It's a sad day," Lewis says. "Mom's going to be sad."

Doug and I glance at each other.

"Yes," says Hilary again. "It might be sad. You might feel sad, too. But it might be very lovely as well."

Lewis nods.

I look again at Doug, who is looking at me. He moves his hand to his stomach. I don't know if he's telling me to breathe, or if he's saying that Lewis has got him again, right there.

By the time I am on my way back to the house after the crematorium, the world seems to have contracted and contracted. I look out the window of the special car I have been assigned by the undertaker, the car that declares I am grieving, I am grieving – and everything seems miniaturised, moving as if speeded up, moving away from me like I'm in a tunnel.

Doug holds my hand next to me, and Lewis sits, still as a stone, next to him. My little man.

Doug's hand is sweating. Or is it mine. He spoke beautifully at the service, shaking slightly at the podium. My father had been like his own, he said, like the one he never had. He left it there but the whole story rushed back to me: Doug's hometown, his own peculiar parents who left him and his sister on their own so much of the time. The absolutely disgusting house, the pathological inattention to hygiene, routine. I only ever visited it twice – and the first time we washed up two plates and two cups to use for dinner. Well, they weren't plates. They were baking trays.

Poor Doug, my God. His folks were nice enough, just entirely useless. I looked at him up there and thought that all this has made him a brilliant father – obsessive, yes, in the opposite direction to his parents – but loving, solid, affectionate. Much like, in fact, my father.

My father was the last relative of sorts for Doug too, except for his sister and her family, far away in California. I must remember, I thought, in the midst of all this, that his own parents died within two years of each other, when he was in his late twenties. I was with him when he heard about his mother. His sister rang at about 6 o'clock one morning. He thanked her, hung up, then turned to me, and we made love. He did not, as far as I remember, go to either of his parents' funerals.

All of this came back to me in quick succession, and, as I sat there listening to him, I was surprised by the force of the memories. Especially by the way we responded to grief then – the sex, the mess of it, the intense drinking and eating. There was a time when families formed the core of our conversation together – their troubles, the attendant battles, the recognition of ourselves in our parents.

But no more. Like the intensity, the sex, we lose track of things perhaps.

I tried once again to remember my father's face, but I could only catch it for a moment as I last saw him: dead, yellow-lit. I saw my mother instead, whose close-up face, peering at me, testing me for truthfulness just through a look, never seems as far away.

Now as we pull up to the house I can see several cars already there. I don't even know who's coming except for Hilary and Adam. I think Doug has invited a few people we know. I again feel sick. Of course, none of them will have known Daddy.

As I enter the house, John, my boss, approaches me with his arms out. Everything else recedes as he reaches for me, and catches me in what he no doubt thinks of as a fatherly hug.

"Marilyn, you poor thing," he says, "and so soon. I'm glad I could be here." He pulls away and leads me toward the drinks. "I almost had to be in Scotland for that conference – meditation and mediation, I think, or some such nonsense. But thank goodness I didn't." His hand hovers over the bottles. "Whiskey, please," I say. "Lovely." He pours me a drink and squeezes my elbow as he gives it to me. "Jacqui will be here later. She sends her apologies and love."

Hilary joins us. "Marilyn," she says, "you should eat something." She takes my arm and leads me into the kitchen.

"Thank you."

"That's okay. You looked like you needed saving. Who's that?"

"My boss John. He means well, he's just –"

"Overpowering."

"Yes, and I must admit a bit of a bore. Apparently we have the pleasure of his wife's company later. Now she's a piece of work."

Hilary sighs. "God, all you need. Now –" she hands me a plate. "I was actually serious. You should try to eat."

Doug finds me in the middle of my sausage roll. "Thanks Hilary." She tactfully leaves.

I look at Doug and try to smile. He looks worn out already. "I see John made it," he says.

"Yes. And apparently we are to expect his wife later."

"Oh. Jacqui."

"That's right. She is forever making me feel stupid and ugly – it's awful how some women do that..."

"I won't give you your own advice and tell you that that only you can make yourself feel that way, that she can't–" I try to glare at him, "—but I will say that Charles and Suzanne should be around sometime, and you can count on them to save you, anyway."

"Oh good." The sausage roll is fuzzing up my mouth, but I mean it. I like them enormously. Suzanne worked with Doug – another electrical engineer. We'd been to their house once for dinner soon after we'd arrived here from London. They'd been back to us once at the old house, and we'd enjoyed it. I kept wanting to get them over again but there seemed to be something in the way – perhaps just too much reservation, too much business. I suspected, however, that it was something else, something not mentioned: that they desperately wanted, but could not have, children. I can see them now in the split second of Lewis waking-up while they were at ours, him walking into the dining room behind me, their faces caught quite bared as if from the flash of a camera, one instant. Especially Suzanne. I couldn't identify the look, didn't know at first that Lewis was there, thought it was Doug, somehow coming in from the kitchen. It was almost greed, the look on her face, or even more primal, hunger – then something else slipped over, and she said, "Hello there, young man." She was another American, although altogether more Southern, being from Virginia. Charles was her perfect complement – smooth, charming, devastatingly handsome and modest, British.

I finish my sausage roll. "It's been ages since we've seen them. I'm glad they're coming."

"Yes." Doug comes over and wraps his arms around me. "You're doing brilliantly," he says. I put my arms around him and rest my head on his chest.

"Thank you. You too. I thought you did just great at the service."

"Thanks."

We stand there a moment. I find that there's something inside me scrabbling around, something trying to protect itself. From what? I think for a second about it. From not feeling anything for Doug right now, from being numb? Again I remember the sex we had after his mother died. I want it, I realise, I want that release. But not with him, and I don't know when this happened or why.

He squeezes me and I squeeze back, then we pull away from each other. "We better be sociable," he whispers, and kisses me on the forehead. "I'll go first."

He leaves, and I continue to stand with my back to the window. The sun comes through onto the floors and wall above the cooker; it's very yellow now, later in the day, and I look at it striking the robin's egg blue we painted the kitchen, the first room in the house we did. My stomach turns, just a little. I can't think why we chose such an insipid, passionless colour.

Back in the throes of the so-called party, someone pours me another whiskey. I've never been much of a whiskey drinker, but my father was, and the feeling of drinking like him is quite pleasant. Added to this is the feeling that no one knows I am drinking his drink, and it feels like my own private accolade.

I sit down on the sofa. I don't sink, or recline, or thud. Just sit. Never carried away, never tortured, or, for that matter, ecstatic. My wedding day. The birth of Lewis. Even grief doesn't seem to disturb the graph of me, no towering peaks or bottomed out troughs. Dad always did say that there was something cold about me, something too analytical. That made me go on to do what I do, but also made me, he would say, hold back. Like your mother, he would go on, God rest her.

Not a wholly bad thing, then, I think now. The whiskey, oddly, seems to be leading me into this kind of distance. There is a mellowness, but also a kind of control with it, a sharpness. Or perhaps it is all an illusion, I wouldn't know.

What I do know, even in this state, is that somewhere all this will come out, probably in my dreams. I feel myself smile and hope no one sees. Someone – I should know who but don't – is talking to me. I try to focus on her. Good grief, is it really a neighbour? The feeling I have that Doug has called in the troops, so we won't be alone, is reinforced. Yes, I think it's Margaret from two doors down. Her voice carries on animatedly, but we are both aware she isn't saying anything important. Meanwhile, I wonder about what's happening inside me, think, my father has always been right about me, always: I determine everything, and allow few surprises. Which comes first, I wonder, the emotion or the reason, the reason or the emotion. Just exactly which one needs to be at the helm?

I can see Doug across the room doing a much better job of mixing this party than I could ever hope to do, even when sober and comparatively untroubled. He looks contemplatively jovial, restrained yet kind, as he is. John's Jaqui has arrived, and

I can see Adam's back, head slightly forward, listening to her. No doubt his attention is well taken by her excesses. She always seems to have something right at the top of her mind which simply must spill out. In my inebriated state I allow myself the thought that John should have counselled her out of her incessant talking and extroversion long ago; it's so obvious she is desperate for validation – surely this can't be attractive to live with? Unless, like so many other couples... I find that I sigh right in Margaret's face, then apologise. I can't even follow through the thought. Who knows what happens in private?

I glance again toward Jacqui and Adam, the back of his head. The nape of his neck is olive, dark like he's been in the sun, and his dark hair spreads in sparse outcrops down the prominent muscles of his neck. The twin indentations on either side of these remind me of a child's head, his own boy's perhaps, or Lewis' when he was a toddler.

I take a stinging sip of my drink, and rest my head on the back of the sofa. A wave of tenderness passes through me. I realise that I don't know what Lewis will be, a giver like Doug, or a holder-back like me. I don't even know what it is best to be, what I would wish upon him.

Lewis. I make my excuses to Margaret and slip out of the sitting room; it's in a bit of a bustle, people loosening up, laughter – and make my way upstairs. For some reason I need to see Lewis, his face. Yet another downfall of an only child, as if we needed any more: the constant worry over his welfare, his happiness and health. But, alarmingly, he seems to know more than I do in some way; even he knows that everyone must die. It's just that I sometimes find myself overtaken by fear, the fear of him dying before me, before his time. My only blood relative. Then I really would be alone, completely alone. I don't think there could be a feeling worse than that.

As I walk, the floor dips like I'm on a boat. I can't remember the last time I was so drunk in the daytime. Hilary will tell me off. A sausage roll is not enough.

I approach his room and I can hear them talking, he and Aaron, I think. There is the clatter of vehicles running into each other, and the high cries of pretend people in trouble. "Oh no-o-o-o-o!" Lewis moans, and as I round the corner I see a miniature man dive bomb a truck and struggle with it. "Dead," Lewis says with finality.

He looks up at me. "We're just doing this, Mom," he says, "aren't we, Aaron."

"Yeah." Aaron looks around. "Look, Marilyn, there's a huge pile-up, and everyone might be dead."

50

"Yeah," Lewis continues, and they are back in their own game. He reaches for his fire engine. "And there might be a fire...nee-naw, nee-naw, nee-naw..." Both boys bend their heads together and start negotiating a path for the fire engine.

I take a step backward out of the room. They are fine, of course, I knew they would be. It's an irrational feeling, an irrational worry, his sudden disappearance. I feel tears coming into my eyes again, and back further around the corner, lean on the wall. Bloody hell. I put my hand over my mouth so they can't hear me. I must be drunk.

I glance over to the stairs and see someone's head ascending. It won't be Doug, I know, he wouldn't leave the party when I'm not there. It's Adam, and when he sees me, he quickens his pace, comes up and puts his hand on my shoulder. Although I barely know him, I put my head down and lean into him. I am extraordinarily tired, exhausted. I really just need to rest.

He moves his hand up to the back of my head, my neck, rubbing gently. Close as I am to him, I can smell his deodorant, or what I take to be part deodorant, part him. It smells wonderful, sexy, and at the absolute second I register this, he leans over and kisses me on the lips. Something happens, and I seem to lose all will; I fall against him – I can feel, briefly, lightly, the outline of his thighs, his erection, and the imprint my breasts make on his chest.

The next second though, I have put my hands up and pushed gently away. I am still dizzy. Adam moves his hands along my arms and takes my hands. We squeeze.

"That was a bit silly of me, wasn't it?" he says. "I'm sorry. My fault. Bad timing —" He pauses. "Or perhaps there's nothing to be timed..." He lets the sentence hang, waiting, no doubt, for some sort of response. The truth is, I know, that an affair with him had never even occurred to me. So the question of timing, as he guesses, is indeed irrelevant.

But I can't deny the charge. It is a charge, I assume, that any stranger kissing me would have created, but it's there. So, I think, I am still alive.

To him I say, "Never mind," and realise almost immediately my mistake. Belittling, to say the least. "I'm flattered," I add, "but it's not a good idea, really, is it?"

He lets go of my hands and pushes my hair back, quickly, gently. "I'm sure you're right," he says. Then, "The boys okay?"

"Yes, in there," I say, gesturing around the corner. "Playing wonderfully together. They're good mates, aren't they?"

Adam smiles, I wonder if it's a little wistfully, but again I feel drunk enough to think anything. He holds out his arm and I take it. "Good then," he says, "shall we go downstairs?"

Somewhat jarringly, Hilary is coming up just as we are going down. I let go of Adam's arm – too quickly, I think, too late – and move a step down from him.

Her voice, however, is bright enough. "There you are," she says, "how are the boys?"

"Fine," Adam and I say together.

"That's good." Hilary doesn't look at Adam, but reaches for my hand. "Marilyn, Doug's been looking for you. People called Suzanne and..."

"Charles."

"Charles, right, are here and want to see you."

"Oh good," I say, "I was hoping they'd make it soon."

We go down and walk across the sitting room, Hilary still holding my hand. It feels quite odd, to be holding hands with someone of my own size. For years that space has been occupied by baby/toddler/child, enclosed by mine. Or held by Doug's, my fingers pushed a little too far apart for comfort. Now – but I don't have time to think about it properly, as I am safely delivered to Doug.

As soon as I join them, Suzanne turns her striking face to me and stops the conversation. Doug touches the small of my back. Suzanne reaches for me and hugs me, her bobbed dark hair pressing against my cheek. And, to my surprise, an unmistakable bump presents itself.

I step back. "You're pregnant," I blurt out, "congratulations!"

She flushes. "Yes. Thank you." She glances at Doug. "Only sixteen weeks. Nobody at work knows..."

"My lips are sealed," Doug says, and he pulls his finger across his mouth as if zipping it up. "Great news," he adds.

"Yes." Suzanne nods. "And we never...," she looks down, then shakes her head a little. "Sorry. It's not important, all over now." She touches my elbow. "But it's you," she says, "we need to be thinking about now, how are you?"

"Oh..." Suzanne looks so radiant, so open. She's older than I am but I feel like an old hag – cloudy face, soft neck. I smile. She would die if she knew what I was thinking. It is part of her charm, her complete modesty.

Suzanne's face has a look of concern. "Doug, get her a drink and something to eat," she says, a little sharply. "Poor thing." She leads me over to the sofa and pulls the small table over. "Damn men, can't see what's right in front of their faces."

Doug arrives, for some reason a little flustered, and Suzanne spreads the food out on the plate. I take a bite of quiche and it's fantastic – who made this? I wonder – and a bit of potato salad.

Doug is still standing. "Can I get you something, Suzanne?" She looks up at him, and I am struck by how familiar they are with each other, how well they seem to know one another. "Yes please, Doug. Something to eat, and apple juice." She doesn't even say another 'please.' Not obsequious at all. Of course they see each other every day, hour for hour more time together than Doug and I have.

Her hand is resting on her tummy. She follows my eyes down. "I keep thinking I feel something," she says, "I know it's silly."

"No, it's not." Before I can stop myself I reach out and put a hand on top of hers. "I started feeling Lewis at fourteen weeks. Like little bubbles, I remember it clearly."

We take our hands away, but I continue looking at her stomach, the small rounding out of it, like a planet, one side of the moon. Being pregnant with Lewis seems a lifetime away now, as of course this life would have seemed then. As Dad dying would have seemed.

I sigh. The reinfusion of a little whiskey begins to take effect and that, combined with the food, improves my spirits in general.

Doug comes back with Suzanne's food and drink, and he sits down next to her, probably for the first time in hours judging by his groan as he stretches out.

It's a small sofa, but we sit wordlessly on it. I look up at the clock – late afternoon. What have people been doing? The noise level has diminished, but even so I am amazed at people's stamina for a party. And a wake at that. There's Charles charming Hilary, who looks more animated than I've seen her in the short time I've known her. Charles is gorgeous, this cannot be denied: tall, blonde, elegant, womanly almost, with a dry sense of humour and perfect white teeth. He too must be delighted with their good news.

After a minute they seem to reach a lull in their conversation, and they turn their heads toward us. I catch Hilary's eye; she raises an eyebrow, and touches Charles' elbow. They move in our direction.

"Hi, Charles," I say, and reach up for his arm. "Great news."

"Yes." He glances at Suzanne. "We're looking forward to it."

I look at Suzanne, too. She has turned her head slightly away, looking at I don't know what, over the high arm of the sofa. There follows the kind of moment I remember experiencing only a few times in my life – an odd gap, a sort of emptiness, yet it is tremendously full of something, something no one knows, perhaps a secret – a space where no one will jump in, and any movement, any word, feels like it might change the course of something, of life maybe, forever. Somehow, we just need to wait for it to pass, hardly daring do anything, and yet each second is magnified, glossy, frozen into frames.

My brain, however, continues its predictable ticking and analysing. Of course these sorts of sea-changes don't really happen, they can't. Cells and momentum – the motion of things – can't change direction that fast, can't change direction at all really. Rather, they do a slow, wide turn, like a ship negotiating wind and current.

Nevertheless, in that moment, I wonder if the feeling I have is right, that something opens up, something perhaps closes. And could it be happening for everyone? I look around, my neck oddly stiff. Slowly, slowly, we bump over, we leap together. Then Charles moves, squats down next to me: "How are you, Marilyn?" and Hilary, I see out of the corner of my eye, picks up my empty glass, makes off with it and hers toward the drinks.

Doug turns to talk to Suzanne. His whole body turns away from me in fact, just slightly sideways, and as I take notice of this, Charles reaches for my hand. I look at him. I do not remember his eyes as so – serious? Beautiful? Or perhaps I've just never looked at them.

The room still has the remains of something unusual, like an echo or a summer storm approaching. Hilary comes back with my drink and slips it into my other hand. Charles' mouth is moving. I can't make out what he's saying. But I have the feeling that whatever it is, it won't matter until tomorrow, or even, much later.

That night, I lie in bed and think of all the countries and peoples in trouble. I don't know why this happens, but it is like a channel which sometimes opens, the swirl of a ham radio. I imagine the darkness overhanging half the earth, the satellites up there passing messages. The conversations people are having, long-distance loves, like a soppy movie, the man and the woman, woman and woman, man and man, hanging onto a piece of plastic, for every word through the crackle and delay. Or indeed the arguments, the phone left hanging there, the misunderstood sentiment, the phone slammed down. Or the conversation that never really begins, but instead runs over and over the same tracks.

And beyond that, there is a quieter hum, one I've experienced all my life, that only comes with my head on the pillow, awake, and only when I'm very tired. I hear voices, people talking, a sort of murmur, some in English, some in languages I don't even understand. Whole exchanges, or just a word. As I grew older and trained, read all my books, I wondered if it was just an expression of my own subconscious, sorting things out. But there's no rhyme or reason to it, nothing changes. It's like I am a conductor for something, a way for people to talk, a receptor. Or it's just a way for me to listen. It is always very calming, comforting, although I long for some piece of clear information, something I can use and gain from to come to light. It never comes of course; the voices bubble on, talking almost without words, and I'm just on that frequency, picking up a few of the crossings and mis-crossings and single messages that go up like flares, a quick burning, *help me.*

I remember a half-conversation with my father about this phenomenon. I suspect that for all his jolly manner, he was fundamentally contemplative, but this never showed itself much, I don't know why. We very rarely seemed to finish a discussion.

He certainly, however, had the air of someone who didn't quite manage to do what he'd intended.

We were on the front porch, where most exchanges with my father happened. At that time of day. I believe it was between high school and college, deep summer. The cicadas were warming up to their racket, and he almost had to raise his voice to be heard. "Like people," he said, "all talking at once!"

I smiled. He would know. His lifetime career, starting soon after he settled with my mother, was working for the phone company, Bell Telephone, or 'Ma Bell' as he called it. "Do you ever think about all those lines, all those people and what they're saying?" I said.

"Sure." He put his drink down on the side table. He gestured with his hands – "You open that box, it swings open like this, and inside are wires and wires of all different colours, each one of them carrying someone talking to someone -- or each one of them might be doing that, could be." He glanced at me. "Because it's unlikely they'd all be in use at once, of course – the system'd probably collapse! Anyway," he went on, "it's the idea that there is ever that much to say, and that I could just plug in and listen to any one of them. Not that I ever did, and the trouble you'd get into if anyone ever found out..." He shook his head. "But I often thought about what this kind of communication could do to peoples' minds, how different people seemed to be from when I was growing up. Their expectations and such." He stopped, abruptly.

"But you don't really do that kind of stuff anymore, do you?" I said, eager to keep him going.

"No," he sighed. "I'm more in the office now, which I don't like as much, to tell the truth. But, as your mother would say, needs must." He smiled at me. "Anyway, I had my time, and it was hard work, out and about in all weathers."

"I can imagine," I said. Then I don't know why I said it, but I did. "I have this thing sometimes," I said, "it's weird. When I hear voices at night, just talking away..." I looked over at him. For a second he stared at me quite intently, then he turned his head back toward the street, where just at that moment a kid on a bicycle rode by.

"I used to have that," he said, matter of factly. "I think I know what you're talking about. And this was even before there were lots of telephones, these big exchanges. There were radios, ship's radios, police talking to each other –"

"But it's more than that," I interrupted.

"Yeah, it is." He locked his fingers together and sat back. "It is. I know what you mean." He shrugged. "I really don't know what to tell you, I've never known what it is. For a while there was something about it that made me want to do something different, make something of myself."

"But you have," I said.

He put his hand up and laughed a little. "Thanks, but I know I'm doing okay. It's just that at first I wanted to do something really big – I used to be an inventor of sorts, I bet you didn't know that."

I shook my head.

"I wanted to make something that would change the world."

"Like what?"

"Well." He laughed again. "That was the problem. It seemed like everything I thought of had problems, didn't do what I wanted, wasn't enough. This was before the war, you know, when I was even younger than you. Anything seemed possible then. Then I met your mother, and life took over. In a nice way, mind you, it wasn't bad." He looked over at me again. "We had you, and a good job seemed the most important..."

"Do you regret it?"

He shook his head. "No, no. You can't have regrets in life, serious regrets. We are lucky to be in this world at this time, so much is happening. We're just running to keep up with progress, with all the new things. I'm getting up there, but I think I do alright. I've had a good life, so far." He held up his crossed fingers.

We both smiled. "Well, I think you've done great." I meant it. He seemed to believe in the future more than I did, even then. "I just hope I do as well and am as happy as you are."

"You will," he said. "Believe me. You'll do better." He waved away my objections. "The point is, sweetie, you should do better, it's the way of the world. Children should always better their parents. And you're a good kid. You will."

It was the end of the longest and most profound conversation I ever had with my father. Soon after, my mother called us in for dinner, and we went in without another word.

My father's face. He was right about so many things, about progress, about almost everything becoming possible. What he ended-up being wrong about was something I could never even mention to him, and now of course, never would. And that is, that one generation does not necessarily improve upon the other, that the great forward motion of his parents and of his own pursuits have more or less stopped with me. My own happiness does not exceed his; indeed, I doubt if it even matches what his was. And for this, as well as for many other things, I know I've gone all wrong. Not so as many people would notice, but enough to feel it tonight, Doug snoring next to me. Enough so that I can't help but think of Suzanne, her beatific face and a new start. Hilary's offer of friendship I don't know what to do with. Whatever it is that keeps me from just seducing my husband. And most importantly, what I know already I won't be able to give Lewis, the sense that anything is possible.

I can't think too much about this now. Not after today. The big thing's been gained – at least I've located my father's face as I want to remember it: healthy, smiling, his lovely hands moving, his hair just turning white, touching his collar, the points of his casual slacks lined up with the toes of his home shoes. At last I have something to hold onto. And so I hold it, push the voices out and out of my head, turn over, and let myself fall asleep.

Monday

Lewis comes in and snuggles up with us earlier than usual. I am in the middle of a deep, hot sleep, and turn away from him, cling to the side of the bed.

My boss John is in my dream, and oddly, Suzanne, who stands in the doorway, holding her enormous belly. I am overcome with rage – she looks so self-satisfied, so Madonna-like, challenging me. She stands so I can't get past: the light is behind her and John is in there, waiting for me. I'm going to be late, and he won't know the reason why. I look down to find I am wearing a suit I don't even own, charcoal grey, with a red shirt, conservative and hard. I feel helpless, and walk over to the window. Outside, two floors below, it is somehow midday, and I can see people walking, toiling slowly in the sun, like they're working in the fields, bent over. My own hands on the windowsill look old, a fine web of lines like gauze laid over the fingers.

I wake to hear Lewis whispering that it's time to get up. "What can I do today?" he says, "What time is it?"

I turn over, reach out for him, find his tummy with my eyes closed. "I'm at work today, darling. You're going over to Aaron's, how's that?"

"Alright," he says, sounding doubtful. "What time do I go? What time is it now?"

Doug moves. "You go at nine," he says. "It's only six thirty now."

I close my eyes again. I should have had another half hour of sleep; already I miss it. I still feel shattered from Friday, even after a slow weekend. And today is my first day back, the first day when I can't think about myself, trace my own patterns.

"Am I going to be there all day?" says Lewis.

"At Aaron's? Pretty much all day," I say. The image of John, moving around in what I now realise is my office, comes back to me. What on earth could it mean?

"How weird," I say out loud. "An anxiety dream about work. About your work too," I add, "Suzanne was in it."

"Humph." Doug grunts disinterestedly and rolls out of bed. Dreams have never been his scene. He barely remembers his, and doesn't even perceive what are to me stunningly obvious waking life connections. But his lack of introspection does tend to save me from myself, upon occasion. Like now. I roll out of bed as well.

Hilary, bless her, says she will keep Lewis overnight so that Doug and I can have a private dinner. I feel guilty – Lewis is not entirely convinced about spending all day there in the first place, might be upset about Dad, who can tell? But I agree. Doug and I haven't sat down together, really sat down, in what seems like weeks – not even since Dad died. And sex – Hilary seems to know this by the look she gives me – it's been in many ways the last thing on my mind. Yet I know I want something, have done for some time – like in the dream, the rage is almost sexual, it is a rage against something, these rooms, whatever keeps me from being what? Who I want? Who I thought I was? Doug and I used to have a wonderful sex life. We just need time to get it back again.

The day is hot like my dream predicted, but nothing else about it really seems applicable. John welcomes me with open arms; and my first client is not some heavily pregnant blonde blocking the way to my true purpose. Of course.

My first appointment is actually someone who should have stopped coming to see me long ago – but she can't quite tear herself away, it seems. Our Monday mornings have become like coffee breaks, while we (she) chats over the events and feelings of the last week. It's a friendship of sorts, a one-sided one of course, and the confusion of roles has recently begun to disturb me.

The morning's diatribe revolves, as it frequently does, around her ex, Matthew. He doesn't call her or he does call her. Today she hears about him in the town with another woman. Not that she minds of course, she expects and even wants him to see other people, and they are divorced, but she feels she should have been told. It's to do with her feelings being hurt, having to find out through someone else. And the other woman, she stresses, she actually vaguely knows. She's very pretty, completely different-looking, blonde, she says, dyed blonde, she emphasises.

"Right," I say. "And what do you think about that?"

"Well, it's like he made a mistake in the first place," she says, "by marrying me. Like he never really liked me how I was, am."

"Yes – but it sort of was a mistake, wasn't it? It didn't work out..." I wait for her to take the bait.

Her eyes fill, and she leans over for a tissue. "Of course, not all of it was a mistake, I know that. There were some good times." She glances up at me, her expression more resigned and aware than her tears suggest. "As they say," she says, smiling a little at her own drama, "there were some good times."

She flops her arms out to either side of her on the sofa. "Bloody hell," she says, "look at me! Ten years later..."

"Well...we've talked about how these things might relate to your parents' relationship."

"Yes." She sighs. "I know the whole thing by now." She gives me a sharp glance. "Of course, I bloody well should!" We both laugh a little.

Her time is almost up. She sits back. "It's funny, you know. Matt in so many ways was just nothing like my father. My father was always a bit of a mover and a shaker, wheeler-dealer type. My mother should have been able to sniff him out, she wasn't stupid. I guess the similarity in the relationships is really between my mother and me, how we both just couldn't see them coming."

"Right," I say, "but that has to do with expectation, with needing something that is invisible, unknown even, to be filled up, taken care of."

We fall silent for a minute.

"But isn't that love?" she says.

"That's part of love," I reply. "But when you need too much to be filled in, completed, it becomes a different thing – it becomes impossible, full of compromises you can't understand."

"Exactly," she says. "You're right. I kept wondering why I was taking this behaviour from Matt: his silences, his refusal to talk to me –"

"Just as your mother, may I point out, 'took' your father, but with different unbearable disappointments."

"His jack-the-lad-ishness," she says.

"Yes."

I look at my watch. "We need to stop now," I say, "sorry."

"That's okay." She runs her fingers through her hair. Quite a handsome woman, I've always thought, only 30, old before her time. Chin-length hair, auburn, slightly hard blue eyes. In the last two years, she'd developed a boyish style I rather liked: trousers, flat shoes, short jumpers, smart blazers. She was quite together really, except for this circular thinking about men. Her excess of need, her assorted and out of proportion expectations. But even these things she handled better than she thought she did. At least she wasn't in a relationship acting it all out, over and over. Slowly she would chip through everything.

She would certainly enter her final relationship a good deal healthier than I did, that was certain.

As I watch the back of her go through the door, I imagine her at work. Her co-workers probably think of her as a little withholding, very private. The un-PC men will talk of her as frigid, while the PC ones will probably fancy her rotten, as they say.

In the time I'm supposed to be filling in my notes, I find myself thinking about my dream again. There's the odd, dominant image of Suzanne, whom I really barely know, and the rather shadowy, background figure of John. A father figure perhaps? In my office, that is, somewhere very close to me, close to the image and construction of myself...my father in my office? No, that doesn't seem right. And this violent red beneath conservative grey. Now I can make a guess at that: sex of course, strapped-in passion. This is true, and the alien feel of the grey suit on my body is also true, the fact that it isn't me, but I'm wearing it, and it seems appropriate to be wearing it. Etc. But I can't get further than that.

I put my pen down and go out to collect my next client. Her first visit. She sits in the farthest seat, hands crammed into a purple silk scarf resting on her lap. "Mrs Jackson?" I say. "Come this way."

She stands up, and, without looking at me, glides like a ghost past me and into the room.

Sometimes the weight of people talking all day becomes like a kind of silence; it presses in like white noise, like I have sat all day on my own in the room.

As I drive the twenty minutes back through town to get home, I try to recover from such a day. A full one, some of my cancelled appointments from last week rescheduled to today. And every single one of them women. Indeed, there is more even than that to say: every single one of them women of a certain age, between about thirty and forty-five. I don't even want to think about why, but I know at least some of the reasons − more likely to seek help, children now at school or out of the house, and the questions held at arm's length until now come tumbling in: who am I? Who is this stranger I have married?

My fingers drum the steering wheel. I stop it and stretch them out. Relax, I tell myself. None of this is news. This is all old, worn stuff. And I just catch it, each story as moving as the last and the next, this awful struggle, the past re-enacting itself, the present imposing, and the future stretching out like this damn road, the views we keep missing.

So. I pull into our driveway, slowly over the gravel. I shake my head a little, look at my watch. Six o'clock. Doug won't be home for a half an hour, and by then I should be cleared out – changed, dinner on. Some slinky number. Not as pathetic as I once thought, back in my college days. They have their uses.

I get out of the car and slam the door. You can barely hear it above the traffic, and I look up at the sky. A yellow grey, approaching a summer's evening. Somewhere else, out in the country, it will be beautiful, seen from all angles, the slightly hazy light refracting, the silver green of the trees in full leaf. I think, tomorrow it's going to rain. Not for the first time I wonder why we work in the summer. Instead, we should sit out, read books, go for walks. There is something quite perverse about working year round, through the seasons, through the changing lengths of days, separating ourselves more and more completely as we get older from any notion of change in ourselves, of growth.

I think of Lewis as I walk in. Poor child. I see him as he often is, in front of his dad's computer, in front of the TV. Not to excess, but enough to miss something, surely. Already it starts. I can't even think, suddenly, if he has walked through the woods in all seasons, or along the nearby beach.

I hang up my coat and walk into the sitting room. For once, I remind myself of my father, how he was always pulling my mother and I along on the weekends – we needed to get *out*, we needed to *do* something. I want to laugh, but don't. The problem is, as soon as we feel something, we want everybody else to feel it as well: the pressing in of age, loss of days. Yet I remember as a child thinking that I noticed more in my melancholy way than my father ever would. I wonder if Lewis will feel the same, if what sometimes looks like aloofness now is really a preparation for his own kind of understanding.

The message light on the answering machine is flashing red. I press the button, and after the beep Doug's voice comes out: "Hi. It's me. Listen, there's a bloody..." I can hear him reach for something, "the deadline for this presentation has been moved forward. I think I'm going to be really late, I'm sorry. Don't worry about dinner, I'll get something here. Sorry. Hope your day went okay. 'Night to Lewis."

I sit down hard on the sofa. Piss. I am crashingly, surprisingly to me, disappointed. Of course, he doesn't even know about having dinner together. Perhaps if I ring him... no, he sounds stressed, not worth the guilt really.

Well that's that. Dammit. I know it will happen another time, we can make it happen another time soon, but the wonderful surprise of it is gone, the gift of it I suppose.

I don't know what to do. I decide to take a shower anyway, change into something comfortable. Then I phone Hilary. She can bring the boys back whenever. Then I think, what the heck. I tell her, let Aaron spend the night here. I've been deserted, come on over for dinner.

A half an hour later, Hilary shows up with the boys and their bags. She kisses me.

"Where's Adam?" I say.

She shrugs. "Called out. I left a note but there's no telling how long he'll be."

I kiss her back. "Oh well. Nice to see you at least."

She pulls out a bottle of red wine. "Thanks. We can enjoy ourselves anyway, even if our other halves are party poopers, right?"

We manage to get the boys into their room fairly early, with promises of parks and doughnuts in the morning. We can still hear them running around, giggling, upstairs by the time we sit down for a drink, but they know they are to stay upstairs on pain of death, so we collapse. Without food we are very quickly, very happily, a little bit pissed. My disappointment dissolves, and

I decide that Hilary is probably better company than Doug would have been in any case.

After a while it's time to get on with some food. We go into the kitchen; Hilary sits at the table. I've already prepared some bits and pieces, so all I have to do is throw them in a pot and stir, cook pasta. I start mixing. Behind me, Hilary sighs. "Thanks for having me over," she says, "it's lovely to be cooked for. That smells wonderful."

"No problem. God knows what it'll be like – my culinary skills stopped developing sometime in the mid-80's." I stop and feed the pasta, linguine, into the boiling pot. "Anyway, to tell the truth, Doug does most of the cooking." I turn back to her to see her reaction.

"Really?" she says, sounding genuinely surprised. "I wouldn't have taken him for a chef. Someone who likes to eat, yes..."

"His paunch you mean?" I giggle.

Hilary resists the urge then goes on. "Well...he's very squeezable. No, I mean you just seem like the looker-after. I assumed you did most things."

"Oh. I don't know." Instinctively I feel she's wrong. If anything, Doug's the carer; I'm more inconsistent. I say as much to Hilary.

"Hmm. I'm surprised." She says it, as they say, in the nicest possible way, yet I find myself wondering why she won't let it drop. Surely this isn't her business if I didn't bring it up, and if I didn't ask her advice. "You seem...much more self-contained than him," she adds, "able to cope with life's ups and downs better."

That is right, now. I feel relieved. "Yes, I think that's right," I say. "His background is an unstable one, and there are great big holes in what he can handle, and when."

"A bit like me," she muses.

"Perhaps." I test the linguine. Almost done. She sees this and starts laying the table.

"But he's much more emotionally open than I am," I find myself saying. "I couldn't tell him I loved him for ages, even though I knew I did. And he's so good with Lewis, rolls with the punches, as it were."

She pours more wine. "I have to say I wish Adam were a bit more like that. It seems that neither of us do that sort of thing very well. I sometimes wonder if it's because we're both basically selfish."

I drain the pasta and mix it in the sauce. It'll do. Whether she has deliberately hit the nail on the head to see how I will react, or whether the wine has just encouraged her to strike lucky, I can't deny that I think she's right. Both she and Adam to my mind are both pretty needy people. Whereas Doug and I – neither of us could be counted as needy, for better or for worse.

I dish up. She's waiting for me to say something, or perhaps she's just fallen silent. I carry the bowls over to the table.

"Lovely," she says, and reaches for her glass. "Cheers."

"Cheers," I reply.

We both take bites of the pasta. Hilary makes appreciative noises. It's pretty good, if I say so myself.

We eat for a moment and then she says, "I hope you don't think I'm forward, talking about you and Doug. It's just that your relationship seems entirely different, by nature somehow, than Adam's and mine. I was just curious."

I hold up my hand. "Don't worry about it. I guess we do try to keep things as equal as possible, with varying degrees of success." It does feel rather imposed, though, sometimes, I think, as I hear myself say this. I don't mention it to Hilary, of course – one mustn't betray the inner workings of a marriage to anyone – but ironically I think that this kind of deliberation of decisions and choices makes growing apart as viable as growing together; they are both always possible. My father's old accusation of being too analytical for my own good surfaces once again.

"Did you hear that?" Hilary says suddenly. We both stop chewing.

"Mom!" It's Lewis, calling. I stand up. "Sorry," I say. "Back in a minute." I go up the stairs and find him standing confused in a dark loo. The bulb's out. I replace it and guide him back to bed when he's done.

She looks up at me as I come back to the table. "Bulb gone in the bathroom," I explain. She nods.

"I was just thinking," she says, "about the people you see. They're not crazy, are they?"

"No."

"They're just..."

"At their wit's end, mostly. People come to me either when some one thing is going drastically wrong and they don't know how to deal with it —"

"Like grief, maybe."

"Yes." I pause. "Or when they find that they keep doing the same unsatisfactory thing over and over, the same kind of relationship, being unhappy in the same ways. Even having the same dreams..."

Hilary smiles. "I wish someone had told me that when I first met Adam. Do you know, I dreamt about him every night for at least a month. A little obsessional, wouldn't you say?"

"Not necessarily. Sometimes it's the only way for strong feelings to come out, like we're overloading ourselves with this great rush, and it has to come out somewhere. Come to think of it, I probably dreamt about Doug a lot when we were first together. In one dream I remember we had two children, isn't that funny, instead of one. Two boys."

Hilary looks at me knowingly. "So you want another one, then?"

I stand up with the bowls. "No, no. I'm – we're – way past that now. I think it's what I thought at the time constituted a family, two point five children and all that."

"Right." She nods slowly. "That and the fact that you're an only child yourself."

I am taken aback. How does she know that? Of course, the funeral. "Maybe." I turn to walk to the sink. "How about you?"

Hilary snorts with typical derision. "No way. I only did it for Adam in the first place, not that you'd know that now, the amount of attention he pays Aaron. It's much more inconveniencing and disturbing than I ever thought it would be, having a child. I'm only just now getting my freedom back." She pauses, comes up behind me with some more washing. "Told you I was selfish."

I glance at her beside me. She is looking at me, hard, to see whether I agree. Our eyes meet, and I am struck by the directness of her gaze, the way the brown of her eyes goes on and on. Not in a deep way, in fact they are rather flat, but in an endless way, like she's not really here. She's looking at my eyes too, and I wonder what she sees. Something starts to creep up on me, something I don't particularly like the feel of. She can see right into me, it seems, and I try to fight it. She can see what I don't want her to see, but that I know is true – that we're both selfish, too selfish for the way our lives are constructed. It's just that she acts on hers, and I, I push mine underwater in the hope it will drown. I listen to people three times a week and encourage them not to do precisely what I have done.

My look must falter, but it is she who breaks away first. She returns to the table, silent. There is something going on here I really don't want to know about. But as I stand at the sink and rinse the dishes it flies into my head, and because it just appears there, rising to the surface, I know it's true. Like the voices at night, like the rare moments of my infant intuition: *she loves me.*

My heart pounds. Christ.

I can hear her gather the salt and pepper, the salad things together to bring over. I turn away from the sink, eager not to be there when she reaches it. As we pass each other she comes to within an inch of me. The space between us now seems suddenly infused, meaningful. I feel the prickle of meaning on my skin, across my chest and rising into my hair.

I stand by the table, pick up my glass. "Let's go through."

In the sitting room, I linger by the CDs looking for something innocuous. Hilary circles the room, straightening drinks mats, examining a print. I pull out something, some obscure jazz, and put it on.

Hilary has stopped her wandering by a pair of ceramic pots. "These are gorgeous," she says. "I don't know why I've never noticed them before."

"Yes." My heart – the romantic notion I cannot replace – seems to make a connection to my stomach, which churns once, painfully. "Yes," I say again. "We bought them on our honeymoon at a gallery in the Lake District." I reach out and pick one up. Without asking, Hilary picks up the other. I run my fingers over the rather dusty outside: they are both the same bone grey, blending to blue glazed at the top, refracting light like a kingfisher's feathers. They are made of the same material, fired the same, but in different shapes. However, I know for a fact they will hold the same volume; Doug and I tried it out once, the proof of an optical illusion.

Hilary runs her thumb over the bowl of hers. "Really lovely," she says. "More..."

"Subtle?" I say.

"Yes. I didn't want to put too fine a point on it." She laughs a little. "Yes. More so than anything else here, really."

"I know." I put mine back and she replaces hers. We sit down on opposite sides of the room. "It's bothered me for some time that they no longer really go with anything else in the house." I don't look at her.

The single sax playing now becomes something I recognise but I can't identify it. I feel a yearning for something, and again, that lurch happens in my stomach.

"So," Hilary says. "We're allowed to dream. And the people you see aren't crazy. We've established that."

I smile. Perhaps I was wrong. I relax a little.

She drums her fingers lightly on her chair. "Where's Doug then, the old sinner? He's missing a good night."

I throw my arms out and sigh. "I know. It's so bloody irritating. We just never seem to see each other these days."

"Know the feeling," she says.

"Yes, but...we've always been quite careful about this sort of thing, spending time together. Perhaps it's just Dad, and work, and summer..."

"Getting on top of you," she finishes.

"Yes." I take a drink.

Hilary drains her glass. "Well," she carries on, "I can tell you something for free – Adam and I never see each other. Never have, never will." Her face closes over, and she looks like the Hilary that used to annoy me.

She sees me looking at her. "No good doing the shrink thing on me, Marilyn, I've solved it. I'm not sure that I care anymore. Anyway, I'm making my own life. I've never had a direction about doing anything, not like you and Adam and Doug. It's taken me a long time to get this far, but I'm going to start classes in September."

"Great," I say, really pleased. "In what?"

"Computing, to start with," she says. "Then I'll see what else I like."

"Great," I say again, "well done."

She sits back determinedly. "Adam just isn't the only one who matters anymore."

Adam's face, close and rather gentle, comes into my mind. "But he seems..." What can I say without giving anything away? Although I am convinced there's nothing to give away, there's also no sense risking it. Hilary's alarming habit of finishing my sentences continues. "So nice? Yes, he does. He is, really. But he'd also probably fuck anything that came within arm's length, I imagine."

My ears are pounding with my heartbeat. "I don't think he's that stupid, Hilary."

She shrugs, oddly calm about it. "I'm not that bothered." And she doesn't seem it. "I'll get some more wine, shall I?" I nod, and she leaves the room.

I stand up too, and walk over to the window. The curtains should have been drawn an hour ago, but I can rarely bear to close them, especially in summer. I look out of the window and at my own reflection, feeling almost completely drunk. An odd sadness washes over me for the second time tonight. Hilary's right about so many things, I think, although I don't want to know them: we are getting old, we do all naturally move apart. And the things I once treasured I've now almost forgotten.

The door opens and she comes back in with another bottle and an opener. "I went to the cellar," she says, "I hope you don't mind. I tried to pick a cheap one." She holds up a bottle and I turn around, barely glance at it.

"Fine," I say. It's French, I think, left over from last summer's holiday. Which we aren't taking this year.

I return to my seat. She uncorks the bottle, and comes over to fill my glass. Her leg presses against my knee as she pours, and I am astounded to feel a small burst of something that must be sexual, right there in that spot. It's gentle, not the crashing in, the stifling of boundless passion – but the ease, the certainty of what? I can only think of Lewis, our bodies unquestioningly and uncomplicatedly touching.

The bottle slips slightly in her fingers and she puts it down, but she returns to her seat. The CD finishes.

"Listen. Marilyn." She pauses.

I freeze. I dread what she is going to say. I pray for her to mention nothing, nothing at all.

"I know it certainly isn't my place," she goes on. "But – I'm very fond of you, and I feel I just can't not say something."

She's not finished. I look up at her, daring her to go on. She looks me in the eye. "It's about Doug and Suzanne." She speaks more quickly now as she sees something – what could it be? – shock, relief – spread over my face. "Did you ever think that they could be having an affair?" Her hands work over each other in her lap.

I don't know how to react. This is so not what I expected that I feel positively breathless. I want to laugh. The whole notion's absurd, of course. I take a deep breath and try to control my face.

"I can see how you might say that," I say, "they work together and everything – but, I don't think so."

"I'm sorry." Her fingers free themselves and float up to her hair, lace in the curls. "I know it's not the sort of thing you're supposed to say...it's just that...there was a moment..."

I don't say anything, don't rescue her. If she's talking about the same moment I felt, the one I put down to change – I don't know what I'll do.

"...when I thought I saw them looking at each other."

I put down my glass. "Hilary," I say, and I am aware my voice sounds like I'm talking to a child. "They know each other very well. They work together every day."

"Yes." She takes a breath. "And I'm sorry to keep pressing a point, but there was something..."

No, no, no, I think. The poor woman is in such a state about her own husband that she wants to see it everywhere. "Look. Hilary." I find myself sitting forward. "Just because by your own admission Adam messes around..."

She too is sitting up very straight, and to my amazement, as I watch, her eyes fill with tears. "That's really not at all what I was talking about. That's got nothing to do with what I'm talking about." She blinks several times and the tears clear away. "Believe me, just because you don't know something doesn't mean it can't be true. And vice versa. Just because I think Adam is a philanderer doesn't mean he is. What really is and what we think we know might be miles apart, or right on top of each other. Or anywhere in between. You of all people should know that."

I am stunned. What is she doing? Why is she doing this? A little voice inside points out that I barely know her, that, inexplicably, she has somehow moved right in. Right into our lives, that is.

Doug and Suzanne. What is she talking about? It's the worst kind of paranoia, the idea that men and women can't be friends, that they can't work together and just be friends. The idea that somehow our hormones are uncontrollable, insurmountable. That we are slaves to our desires, end of story.

I glance at her. Her head is lowered, and I can't see if she's crying. She is certainly still, except for those hands going. Of course, I think, she would believe anything could happen, that nothing is outside of possibility, or predictable. Whereas, obviously, I would believe differently. That most things are known or able to be anticipated.

She interrupts my train of thought. "Would you like me to leave?" She raises her head then, and I am shocked by how miserable she looks.

I shake my head. I'm not going to be melodramatic about this. She has a full glass of wine, she can stay. I reach for mine. We are almost in the middle of another one of those moments. I think of the dream I had about my father on that first night, holding something back, forcing something unmentionable behind me and back out the door. Then I think of the dream I had last night, how angry I was at Suzanne, how disappointed in myself. The faint outline of John in my office, against the light. Suzanne prevented me from getting in, but I also didn't want to go that badly, wasn't all that interested. The two dreams seem to have set up something I don't quite understand yet, something about being pulled in two directions, both toward and away from the things that are important to me. And yes, somewhere in there is sex, in both dreams. The sex which needs to be hidden – private, almost sordid – and the sex which becomes public, makes babies, draws people together.

Fuck. I cannot even put Suzanne and Doug in the same room, much less the same bed. The whole thing is outrageous. I can only feel Suzanne's tight roundness under my hand, its promise. Doug's weight on the sofa, Suzanne and I rolling in toward him. Charles' mesmerising face, and the moment when everything seemed to stop, for me at least. Something seems to have revealed itself to Hilary in that pause, but I can't imagine it. Thinking of it now all I feel is tired, older than I thought, ashamed to admit a feeling of past caring. With Dad now gone, with Doug and me...

Of course, Hilary might be right. I look at her again. She has moved back in the chair, her eyes closed. I suppose there might be an external reason for the secret state of my marriage, but the internal workings are all I need think about, really. And internally we could tick along like this until kingdom come. Doug doesn't have it in him to do anything tremendously exciting, and nor, for that matter, do I. It's Hilary and Adam who have something, some kind of harassed, messy, passionate life, surely? And I haven't yet and may never, tip over that balance, take a walk, as they say, on the wild side. Once you go there, I know from my clients, you have a hard time getting back. You almost have to forget you ever left, to ever get back to Kansas.

Hilary feels calmer now, I can tell. I begin to relax a little. We may both be learning something. I admire her in some ways; she's the only live wire among us, the only one of us making some kind of grand attempt against the current. Who knows where she will kick next, and I find myself wishing her all the luck. Put us together, I think, and in some ways we'd be the perfect combination, better than either of our marriages.

The room feels emptied of everything but us, two women in a bit of a mess. I think of all the people who are supposedly close to me: Doug, Lewis, some old friends in the States. Only Lewis seems important, and it's so obvious now that I am already failing him. Perhaps it's because of my genes: their indelible print, their serving of tranquillity bordering on immobility, the automatic observation of every angle of a problem. Or perhaps it's just everything about me.

Poor Lewis. Will he ever dare to kiss a stranger in a dark hallway, like Adam did? I can feel his lips now on mine. An accident, but a pleasant one, rather like the bumping together of docked boats, according to tides and ripples.

Or will he be like Doug, ever safe, ever dependable. Like me too, really. Though not if Hilary is right. Suzanne and Charles, Suzanne and Doug, the two notions mix together and now seem perfectly possible, almost acceptable. If she wants him, she can have him – hell, why not? There's Charles of course, but he's beautiful enough to have his own interests, to cultivate attentions without too much struggle. For all I know this exact scenario has been rocking along for months, and Suzanne's baby is – of course, Doug's, it's quite simple.

Again, I feel a peculiar acceptance about the whole thing. I laugh out loud a little. It feels almost fact now, and strangely it doesn't change Doug's safeness, his solidity. It becomes instead another measure of my failing. I can't handle another child, so he begets another elsewhere. I am unable to love him completely, so he completes himself elsewhere. And all the while he's fine, he's just fine, happy really, fulfilled, satisfied, still every man to every one, his forté.

Well. Hilary is looking at me with something like pity, but perhaps it's sympathy, or the love I was wondering about. She stands up and walks over to me, sits down next to me on the sofa. I feel my heart drop again, only this time it stays down, and an image passes through my mind, so fast I barely think it, but see it: a wrapped body, going through a chute, and sinking unevenly, first the head, then the feet, the head, the feet, through the water and landing on the bottom of the ocean. It's Dad of course, dead, and my own ship carrying on, passed over.

Hilary reaches for my hands. She holds them lightly, her own hands still now for once. I feel a little as if I'm choking, fighting as I am for a full breath. One by one everything seems to have cut loose, or have I cut them. Whatever the case, I feel now the last thing go, whatever it is, and I begin to drift.

Hilary squeezes my hands, spasmodically. My God, I think, she's going to kiss me.

Hilary

Monday

Adam arrives before Doug, a bit of a surprise as I hadn't
expected him to show at all. Rid of the wife and kid, I thought
he would think – whew, nothing better.

But here he is at the door when I go to answer it, the
note I wrote him still in his hand, like he'd been thinking about
something else.

He's surprised to see me, too, obviously, expecting
Marilyn. He leans forward and kisses me, briefly, on the cheek. I
can see he's feeling rather jolly. I wonder if his last call out was
really the child with tonsillitis it claimed to be. Nothing is
impossible anymore.

"Where's the party?" he says.

We turn to walk in, along the high ceilinged hallway,
with its dark green walls. I haven't known them long enough,
Marilyn and Doug, to know who has the eye for colour; I

imagine it is Marilyn. I like their taste, however, by and large, except for the kitchen. As we walk through, I pretend that it's our house, I like it that much, that it's mine. It's a feeling which takes me back to babysitting days, pretending you live somewhere else.

We walk into the room. "Drink?" I say.

Adam stops. "Where's Marilyn?"

I circle round and sit down. Very comfortable chairs as well.

Adam is still standing in the doorway. What's wrong with him? I study him...of course. I should have guessed. Or perhaps I did, and thought of it no differently from any of his other interests. He fancies her like mad, like rotten even. In fact, I would say it's almost got the better of him. That's why he's here.

"Come on, silly," I say. I gesture toward the sofa where Marilyn had been sitting. As he walks over and lowers himself into it, I feel a frisson of what? – danger, sex.

"She's gone out," I say. "She didn't say where she was going, she just left."

"Right." Adam stands up again and pours himself some wine. It's her glass, but he wouldn't know that. I wonder if he can taste or smell her somehow, his lips on the edge pressed over the smudges.

"Did she say when she'd be back?"

"No. She needs —"I rub my thumbs over the tapestried arms of the chair. "She needs space, I think. That was my impression."

Adam seems unwilling to ask more although there is plenty more to tell. He stands up once more, and goes into the kitchen. I can hear him opening cupboards, the clatter of him finding a plate. I presume he scrapes out the last of the dinner, and returns to the sitting room. He seems completely disconnected from reality. Or is it me. Or both of us. My own house – the tea I made for the boys, dishes still unwashed, the dry clothes out on the line, now wet with dew – this all seems a million miles away now, another country.

After a minute or two Adam puts down his empty plate. "I would have thought Doug would be back by now."

"Yes," I say. "Or perhaps Marilyn went over to see him."

"Why would she do that?" Adam says. "When he's coming back?"

I shrug. "I don't know. The truth is, she *was* in a bit of a state."

"Oh?"

"Yes. Doug working tonight was one in a long series of such things, apparently."

Adam is staring off, turning his wine glass around and around. "And I must say," I go on, "I know what that's like."

He glances at me, his face and eyes flat. "Right," he says again. "And I suppose you informed her of this, did you? Christ!" He puts the wine glass down, and laces his fingers together in his lap. He is angry, but I feel oddly exhilarated. His desire for her is plain on his face – the red in his cheeks, set of his mouth, cold in his eyes. He is fighting a losing battle.

"Why can't you keep your nose out of anything," he almost hisses. "The poor woman. She is too nice to you, she really is." Checkmate, sunshine, I think. He's glaring at me, and in that glare somehow I want to screw him. I see the same thing flicker, out of control, across his eyes. The satisfaction is tremendous.

We sink into silence, waiting and not waiting for something, our usual state. Neither of us hears the door until it closes – hard, resoundingly, like someone with his mind made up.

We look at each other. Quite suddenly, I feel sick, all the wine I've drunk sloshing around in my stomach.

And then, as soon as I see Doug I start crying, which irritates me. It's not an all out sob, but a welling-up, a choking up, a bit too helpless and female for me.

He stops and looks around the room. "Marilyn upstairs?" he says, looking tired and confused. "Is Lewis okay?"

"Well, no, actually," says Adam. "I mean, the boys are fine I think." He glances at me and I nod. "Marilyn isn't here. We thought she might be with you."

"Oh. I didn't know you were going to be here." Doug moves back out into the hall to hang up his jacket, placing his briefcase neatly where he always keeps it. He comes a couple of steps into the room then stops again, his hands in his pockets. He laughs a little.

"Well that's unusual, isn't it?" he says.

Adam and I, by now on our feet, guide him to a chair. I go for another glass. I am comforted by how well I know this role. I pour him some wine.

Adam crouches down next to Doug's chair, why I can't imagine. In case Doug flips, I suppose. "What time did you say she left?" Doug asks.

Adam turns to me.

"About nine-thirty," I say, "nine forty-five."

"Nine-thirty," he relays to Doug.

"Okay." Doug sits back, rubs his palms on the arms of the chair. "How odd. It's not like her at all. Sorry about this."

"That's alright," I say, and give him the wine. He takes a big gulp, then sits forward quickly. "God, where's Lewis?" he says.

I point up to the ceiling. "Upstairs. He's still here. She didn't take him. It didn't – " I don't know what to say, whether to say anything. "– it wasn't that kind of thing, something dramatic. She didn't say much."

"Right." Doug stands up. "I'll go check on him."

Adam and I glance at each other. Adam steps forward. "Just look in, Doug, good idea. But maybe it's best to leave him sleeping, you don't want him up now."

"No, no." Doug is moving quickly, at the door already. "No, I won't. Of course you're right. But I need to see him." He turns back to face us suddenly, and looks from one to the other. In that moment I think, oh my God he loves her, he still really loves her. He was happy, really happy, right up to the moment when he stood in the doorway of the sitting room, and found us here. All the way home he was happy, thinking of Marilyn waiting for him, waiting up probably as she usually does. He wanted to talk about his day – he's had a terrible one, people fucking him over right, left and centre. And right up until just that split second, even walking in the door into a silence he wasn't expecting. Right up until that second, everything was A-okay. And now, boom. Like a mirror image of itself, life is not okay. Everything is not – I imagine him repeating it to himself – *not* okay.

Shit. I try to swallow.

We hear Doug's feet on the stairs, going up. "Well," says Adam. "This is one for the books."

I look over at him. His languid way irritates me more than ever, his full lips. I feel the omnipotent anger boiling up – our absurdity together, our emptiness.

"Will you *shut up!*" I say. "Just shut the fuck up."

His manner changes instantly. He leans closer to me: "Look," he says. "I know, I know what this means." He touches the side of his head with one finger, taps it in a crass way. "I know one fuck of a lot more than you think I do."

"Really," I say. I hear my voice, equally as crass, give a juvenile emphasis to the word. What are we doing?

Doug's footsteps creak down the stairs and a second later he appears at the door.

"Okay?" I say.

He nods. "Yes, fine. Sleeping like babies, both of them. God – " He sits down heavily, puts his head in his hands. "This is silly, I should do something, I'm just so tired." He sighs. "Where could she be? I just can't think." He lifts his head up and looks at Adam, who prods himself to life.

"Ummm. Maybe she's just out, you know, maybe she just had to get out. That happens sometimes." He speaks, I can see immediately, from experience.

"Some people, maybe," Doug says firmly, "but not Marilyn. She's not like that. Funny, I remember when we were first going out she used to say to me that if she ever ran away, I should come and get her. I've never understood that, because she's never run away, in all our years together. She's never even left the house in an argument, never." He pauses, and says, almost to himself, "Of course, now I don't even know where to look."

I can hear his voice beginning to crack. Oh Lord, I think, don't start, or we'll never get past this moment.

He doesn't. He straightens up and looks me in the eye again. "In some ways," he says carefully, "it doesn't really matter where she's gone, does it, because she's coming back." I nod. "These things happen in life, don't they?" he goes on. "People change, people go through...crises." I nod again. "Even when people thought they never would." He presses his hands together in front of him, the fingers, palms and thumbs perfectly aligned.

"Yes," Adam jumps in. "You never can tell. You never know what people think they need to do."

Doug nods his head stiffly, like a child does when first learning it, deliberately.

Adam looks at his watch. He raises his eyebrows at me. "Hilary, we need to decide what we're doing. I've got a full house tomorrow. Doug – would you like us to stay?"

Doug shakes his head in that same slow way.

"No? Right." Adam heaves himself to his feet. "Let's take Aaron with us. Whatever happens, Doug won't want to see him in the morning."

I stand up, but Doug doesn't move. I wonder if we should stay, whatever he says.

I walk over to him, touch the back of his chair. "You'd like us to go?" I say. He nods. "Okay." I stand up again and walk over to the doorway. Adam whispers "Aaron," and points upward. He goes out the door and I can hear him shuffling up the stairs.

Doug sits back heavily, and I see embarrassingly bared despair on his face. "Hilary?" he says.

"Yes."

"You spent the evening together, right?"

"More or less. It was a last minute thing."

"Because I couldn't come back?"

"I think so. Not that she said exactly that."

"Did she give any indication of anything? Anything at all?"

"No, not really. We were talking – it was rather intense, but nothing –catastrophic, so to speak. At one point she got up and went into another room, the loo I thought. Then when she came back in, she had her jacket on. She said she was going out. That was it. I didn't feel somehow I could ask her what she was doing or why. I just thought – one of those things."

Doug is looking at me steadily. "Right. And that was it."

"Yes."

"Was there anything in what you were talking about..." I can tell he feels uncomfortable even asking.

"No, no, not really. It was kind of ranging around family and relationships, the usual thing."

"Perhaps her father...?"

"Yes, a bit of that. She has been through a lot recently."

Doug stretches his arms straight up over his head. "Yes, she has." He rubs his eyes. "Christ almighty. She's got to be okay."

I put my hand on his shoulder. "I'm sure she is, Doug, I'm sure she is. She just needs time."

"No point in calling the police," he says rhetorically.

"No. They won't..."

"...do anything yet," he finishes. "I know."

I can hear Adam fumbling with the front door. He seems to have taken a long time; I'm eager to leave. I walk out of the sitting room and see Aaron half-awake over his shoulder. "We need to go now," I stage whisper to Doug. He stands up. "We'll talk in the morning."

Adam, Aaron and I pile into the car and head down the wet streets. I hadn't even heard the rain start, but we need it. The lamps reflected on the streets are almost unbearably bright; I look back and see that Aaron is keeping his eyes shut. We go home in silence, supposedly so as not to disturb him, but I know that's not the reason.

It's making me a little sick, the smell of flowers going over. Marilyn didn't like them in the house, or she had too many, so she gave me some to take home. And now – god, the stench of them.

I open the upstairs windows, lean out the big one round back. It is now one-thirty in the morning, and I can smell the honeysuckle directly under this window, the powerful sweet perfume.

Damp hangs in the air, what will turn into an early morning mist. I feel a sort of elation, the elation of a new love, perhaps. It's the first time I've been on my own, really alone, since seeing Marilyn, and I feel the evening, with a life of its own, close to me, like a baby in a sling. The feeling of having been up half the night, gritty eyes, dry mouth – and yet the sting, the sharpness of the wet grass out there, the quiet branches. It's an old feeling; I can only trace it back to a time when I was alone, my teenage years, when nobody even pretended to know me, but I pretended to myself to be lonely, enjoying being on my own.

This time last week. Last Monday. It seems so strange, I can hardly think about it. This time last week my house, and Marilyn's house for that matter, were ticking along in their zipped up ways, hers better decorated than mine, but mine a little easier to be in, I thought. Anyway, that was only a week ago, when nothing that seems so important now had even entered the scene. Her dad dying, all the flowers, Suzanne and Charles. On her own.

Poor Marilyn. A week ago none of this would yet have happened. Even my flowers, the first to arrive Tuesday night, would still be sitting in their green bucket, ungathered in the florist's. Her father would be thinking what would turn out to be his last thoughts, no doubt about her and Lewis.

My mind shifts down and back to the flowers, the smell of the honeysuckle reminding me. I gave her lilies – beautiful, but with the staining centres I meant to cut out. That Tuesday morning was my beginning into her quiet, dependable life. And now look at them. Look at me.

Well. I saw it. I was there. I saw her face when she got off the phone, the terror. The falling away of the rickety kitchen table where I sat, the brittle plastic nature of everything suddenly – the cheapness of it, of everything.

That's right. Something about her had been cheapened, I couldn't put my finger on it. In that moment and so many moments that week. And no one but me could see it. Last Tuesday, as I went through the rest of my day, something shifted, like a change of wind, like someone had swung my sails and caught me, full on, and I started racing toward heaven knew where. Toward some other shore.

The wonderful lilies. I'd not done anything like that before. Tonight I didn't see them there – were they dead already? I thought it was just carnations, overripe roses, like those in my house now stinking out the place – I thought they went first. I never would have chosen lilies if I knew they'd be the first to go. Nevertheless, the idea of them lying somewhere – in her compost heap perhaps, rotting slowly, becoming the earth – is not altogether unappealing. I take a deep breath. I can almost taste the dirt, the delicious mineral haunt of it, the nearly hidden scent intermingled with the honeysuckle, held on my tongue like a sweet. If they had to go, I think, there are worse ways than that, rotting sweetly.

A few minutes later I go into the bedroom. I think I have been hanging over the open window for quite a while, but Adam is still awake, even though his eyes are closed.

The light's still on. "He go alright?" I say, meaning Aaron. Adam cracks his eyes open. "Yeah, yeah," he says, "no problem."

As I get undressed I am slightly surprised, but gratified, to feel Adam's eyes on me. I pull my trousers off, sliding my hands more closely than perhaps strictly necessary over my hips. I bend over to take them off, one foot at a time.

I've been lucky, I think, as I lift my jumper up. Aaron didn't do much damage, considering. Not, as I said to Marilyn, that I would ever have another one. I feel myself shiver a little, pat my stomach, the skin a bit lax. Carrying a baby is the most peculiar thing in the world, so limiting. Just a vessel for something you don't even know, it gets to the point when you can't even do your own shoelaces up. We end up just exactly how someone wants us to be – helpless. No, I think again, never.

I unclip my bra and peel it off. I've always thought that was sexy, letting the breasts loose. From an image I have of my mother I think, watching her get undressed, amazed at the difference in shape between her natural breasts and the way the bra forms them. I look down at my nipples, dark, little changed by Aaron, thank God. Yes, overall I've been lucky.

I walk naked over to the bed, carrying my nightgown. I pull back the covers, 'accidentally' flipping them too far back. My hunch is confirmed: although Adam's eyes are now closed, feigning sleep, his dick is erect.

I reach for it. He doesn't move. It is completely hard immediately, and I pull it out from his body slightly to see it. Quite a glorious one, in my limited experience, no wonder he needs to follow it so absolutely.

I move my hand along it a little and he opens his mouth to breathe, eyes still closed. So, I think, this is what it's going to be tonight, perfect.

I get on top of him and lean over, let my nipples brush his face. His dick moves in my hand. I raise myself up, and guide the tip around my clitoris in circles. I am already wet, feel as though I've been wet for days, and he slips in easily.

As we start, I begin talking. "You can't come," I say, but as I say it I know he's almost there. "You don't love me anymore, remember. I'm not a good enough fuck." Something else occurs to me. "The truth is – " I pull away from him, and move my hand to myself. In a couple of seconds I can feel the orgasm gathering. "The truth is I don't even need you." And I don't – I come, quickly and painfully, aching for something to be inside me.

He moves his hands up. "Oh no you don't," I say. I want to come again anyway, and I reach down, lower myself on him hard. To his credit, he does fill me. I pull his hands away and move so fast we both come within seconds.

I sink down, still on top of him, covered in sweat. He has not opened his eyes the whole time. I roll off of him, and turn off the light. I think, he's such a sucker.

I am walking down a narrow unpaved road, with dirt where tyres go and something yellow, gold – is it wheat, corn – growing up in a stripe down the middle. And on either side of me too, taller than I imagined, the same yellow or gold plant grows, out almost as far as I can see, to the edge of the field through which I am walking. So I know I am walking through a field, down a road where cars certainly travel, but evidently only sometimes. The sky is a yellow-blue, the bright blue of too much sunshine, the deep of summer, rain needed.

I find myself walking and walking down this path, and as I walk I become aware that I am going somewhere, and this is a relief. Soon a funny house comes into view – a white bungalow with a grey tile roof, surrounded by a stone wall. At first I can't see anything else, just the stone wall, the thin line of white, and the roof above. But as I get closer I can see that it has nice windows, old-fashioned ones for a bungalow, small cottage checkerboard panes.

I walk right up to the iron gate and open it with a metallic clang. I go in, and shut the gate behind. Looking around, I see an enormously colourful and completely unanticipated garden full of high summer flowers: geraniums, delphinium, lavender, lilies, sweet pea, michelmas daisy. There are brick paths through like the sort of garden I used to read about, and the paths wind all around the house, the bottom part of which I now see is covered in ivy.

I join one of the paths and follow it round to what must be the back of the house, if anything can be the back when surrounded on all sides by wall, and beyond that, rows of wheat.

In the back there is a patio, and on the patio is an ironwork table, two chairs, a newspaper on the ground next to one, held down by a rock.

Christ, I think, what am I doing here. I want to get a look at the paper for a clue, but find instead that I am walking toward the other chair. I sit down, and put my hand over my forehead to look up into the sun just as someone comes back out into the garden.

"Oh hello," she says, "I didn't hear the gate. Found it alright, then?"

I open my mouth to speak and something comes out. "Yes," I say, "but it's a bit of a way, isn't it?" I am still looking up into the sun, and although she has stepped between me and it, the light keeps me from seeing who she is.

She leans forward a little and sets something down on the table. As she moves in front of me I see her hair, caught gold.

She pours something cool to drink. I can hear the cracking of the glass as the liquid hits it. "Here," she says, sounding kind but as if she barely knows me. "Have some of this at the end of your long journey."

I take a sip and it really is refreshing. We don't speak for what feels like some minutes, then I say, "Your garden – I didn't know things could grow like this, in the middle of a field, in the same place where the field grows."

She laughs a little, a high tinkling laugh which reminds me of someone but I can't place it. "Where the soil is fertile, my dear, many things thrive. Don't worry about chemistry. All you really need to know is, where one thing grows, another will as well."

I take another sip of my drink, and rise to the surface of my dream thirsty. I sit up in bed, still half asleep, look at my watch, 4 o'clock. I'm dying for water; with all the fuss I didn't have enough to drink before bed. I deliberate for only a minute, then get up, put on my dressing gown. I need to pee anyway.

I go downstairs, the remnants of the dream still with me. How odd to find such a lush place in the middle of a dry, hot summer. Of course, I'd been thinking about flowers, Marilyn's and mine, before bed, that's probably it.

Was the woman Marilyn? I finish my glass of water and close my eyes. I don't see her, I don't even see Marilyn. I hear a voice, but it's not Marilyn's. It's another woman's voice, still with an American accent, but an advertising kind of voice, like an ad for washing detergent.

I open my eyes and run another glass of water for myself. What do I know? The more I try to think about it, remember it, the further away it goes. Like Marilyn, it seems to disappear if you look directly at it. Like her face.

The water now encourages a fresh feeling of drunkenness. Why on earth did I say those things to her? What on earth possessed me? As I stand at the sink I feel myself start to shake all over, tremble even down to my legs, which sway like I'm at sea, back and forth. I hold on to the edge of the counter and wait for it to pass. I think about Aaron, how he needs me. I think about how I can help Doug, and dear Lewis. I manage, for a moment, not to think about Marilyn, her hair caught up uncharacteristically about her face, her changed breathing. What happened or could have happened. And in that moment, I recover myself. I think, I will go to sleep, I will not dream. And before I know it, it will all be over.

Friday

I wake up feeling drugged. Aaron is calling from the bathroom and Adam – I turn my head to look – is up already, or just back from a visit. "Mum!" says Aaron again. I close my eyes. I know it's raining, I can hear it in the sound of the cars going by out front, and in the remaining quiet – no birds, just deadening warm rain.

I roll over and sit up. The rain is now confused with the shower going. Perhaps Adam has atypically come to Aaron's rescue and turned it on for him. Whatever the case, I wish the water would stop – the rain, the shower. I shake my head, trying to clear it. It's the fourth day of rain, and they say there's more to come, one of the wettest summers on record. Across the country crops are being flattened, waterlogged, floods are threatening.

Here, however, I almost wish for something violent instead of this civilised, quite pleasant affair with even the odd rainbow or two. It's been like this ever since Marilyn left. Or 'disappeared.' That's what we keep saying, disappeared. Like it might have been against her will, like she certainly didn't mean it. Might as well say lost, except that that implies not being able to find your way back home. Went out and forgot to leave the bread crumbs, confused the stones with ordinary gravel? I don't know. I do know she could find her way back if she really wanted, or perhaps if she was able. So she's not lost, she just feels that way to us.

God. My stomach churns. Minute after minute I feel sick, from the moment I sit up in bed. I am even dreaming about her, hot and desperate and muggy. I'm dreaming about her every night, I know I am. I can feel her like she's with me, but she's not. I can never see her face.

I stand up. Another wave of nausea. I wonder if I might be pregnant. I repress the urge to laugh out loud. Not only would chance be a fine thing, but – my mind goes blank. It would be terrible news.

I look at the bedside clock. It's late, eight o'clock. Lewis will be here soon, and Doug.

I manage to make some coffee by the time they arrive. Doug and Adam pass each other out back: Adam stops, moves his hand to his head like there's a hat there. Doug is looking down, then quickly up at the sky. He holds up his hand, palm flat. The rain, I know he is saying, good God.

Adam rests his hand on Lewis' head, who wriggles out from under it, his eyes scanning the windows for Aaron. He spots something, and runs in, whizzes past me and up the stairs.

Doug, however, seems stuck. I watch as the drizzle darkens his hair a little, and Adam, for all his faults polite, sympathetic, turns up his collar. He nods toward the house – you better go in. Doug holds up his hands in a kind of apology – I'm sorry, you must be busy. They part, and Doug comes up the drive.

I open the door for him. He almost falls in, and I reach out, catch him, squeeze his arms through his damp mac. He kisses me on the cheek, "Hello Hilary."

He sounds terrible, croaky, and looks worse. Never a very dashing chap, lack of sleep has left his skin grey, drooping. His hair is greying too, more than I'd noticed before, and he's given himself a bad shave.

He sees me studying him and walks past, hands up in a similar gesture of apology. "I know, I know," he says, "don't even talk about it."

"Any news?" I ask, knowing there isn't.

"No." He sits down at the kitchen table as I put the kettle on. I hear his hands slap the table softly. "This all still seems – impossible somehow."

"Yes."

"I phoned the police last night again. They say they are 'on it', whatever that means. No sign yet of anything, though, this is what I can't understand. Not her bag, jacket..."

Shoes, trousers, t-shirt, I think, remembering what she was wearing that night. Green stone necklace.

"In some ways that's good, isn't it?" he says, not expecting an answer. "I know it is. But it's like the ground just opened and swallowed her up, whole."

An awkward silence falls between us. Or rather, the gruesome image does. We both know it might be true, just might. I am by a chair, so I sit down, abruptly.

"But they are working on it."

Doug sighs. "Well I guess so," he says, sounding very vague and American. I've thought this before – regardless of how old they are, American men often just sound like boys, like they're still in high school or whatever it is. Part of the damn football team.

I notice for the first time what he's wearing. "You look smart," I say, "where are you off to?"

"Oh —" he looks down. "I'm going to go in to work for a little while."

"What?!" Before I can stop myself I say it. "Shouldn't you stay home just in case?"

He stays calm. "Well." He wraps his hands around his mug. "They say get on with things. They say I can't do anything more, and with Lewis —" He takes a breath. "You know how it is with kids. No matter what, you just can't stop."

"No."

"Anyway," he continues, "I thought it might take my mind off it all a little, just for a few hours. Suzanne's struggling, apparently..." He trails off.

At the mention of Suzanne's name a strange thing happens to me. I feel something tingly – desire or tremendous anger – rush over me.

"Suzanne." My voice sounds flat. Again, it comes out before I can stop it. You better watch out, I tell myself, watch your step.

He glances at me. "You met at the funeral, didn't you? Woman at work, expecting?"

Of course I bloody know who she is, I think. I nod.

"Married to Charles," I say, "lovely man." Doug looks at me. "He was a sweetie, although −" I stop. "I shouldn't wonder if things are a little amiss between them, the way he was behaving..."

Doug sits back, crosses his arms. "What do you mean?"

I stand up and go listen at the bottom of the stairs. Silence in Aaron's bedroom. "Oh, it doesn't matter," I say, "you would know better. I only met them the once."

Doug is quiet. He gives nothing away, I think, very practised.

"Marilyn didn't think there was anything up either, now I think of it," I say. No reaction from Doug. "It was one of the things we talked about...Monday."

Doug nods. His face is completely impassive. I am amazed at how stony he can keep it, and think, he missed his calling, should have been a lawyer. No wonder he and Marilyn had this, this thing with this quiet centre, deathly quiet I'd say. No wonder they didn't have sex.

Doug seems to be thinking about something else altogether. He turns to me. "I'm sorry to impose on you even more, Hilary, but can you keep Lewis? Just until after lunch?"

"Sure," I say. Doug looks pathetic, torn apart. Split in two, I shouldn't wonder, between wife and mistress. Not ideal, but that doesn't mean this whole thing isn't just horrible. It's surprising what women will go for, though; compared to Charles, Doug is just...stolid.

He stands up. "Thanks." He leans over, a bit of a bear of a man, and hugs me. I am reminded of Marilyn, her frailty next to him. I feel tearful again, and sorry for all of us.

Doug sees my face. Neither of us say anything, and he turns, walks out the door. As I watch him go I know that she loved him. I don't know why, and she was worth so much more, but I think she did. I imagine them at university, a little weight off of him. The way that they are both quiet people. There was probably something there, I decide, but by the time I met her, I could see she was drowning in it.

I stand at the kitchen window for quite a while after Doug disappears through the gate at the bottom of the garden. It is still drizzling, but something in the air feels like it might clear.

I put the kettle on. The boys upstairs are ominously quiet. However, I know if there is trouble to be had it will be Aaron, not Lewis. Lewis the good child. Aaron his father's son. Lewis so like – my throat tightens. Of course, I haven't really thought of it before, how like Marilyn Lewis is. Completely different colouring, but very similar ways: careful, almost studious; an air of nearly always being a little confused or perplexed by life, but willing to make a go of it. Observers rather than participants. What must the child be thinking? What would Marilyn think?

I go back over to the window. This time last week was only the beginning of something I thought would be over soon – for me, anyway. The wake, over by the weekend, my good deed done, my helping Marilyn through the mess of a dead parent.

Both of my parents, unbelievably, are still alive. Still several hours away. Mercifully, Adam would say. And perhaps I agree. They never seemed to teach me much of anything, never seemed to enlighten me to the ways of anything at all. Not for lack of trying, probably, on their part. The truth is I hardly remember a thing about my childhood. We just went along in a kind of semi-amiable truce, surrounded by empty but not disagreeable space. It is true to say that we allowed each other a great deal of space, to the point where even my parents led virtually separate lives eventually, not to speak of my older sister and older brother, seconded into the attic by the time I turned twelve. My mother – same out of control hair as me, same obstinate spirit, blah, blah. And my father, almost invisible, yet with the final word on everything.

I wonder what Marilyn would say about me if she'd known anything about my family. Probably that it's what she suspected, or some such noncommittal thing. She never pried; it was one of her great strengths, knowing when to keep quiet. Really, it was like she could see right through me. As if, indeed, I'd walked into her office. After all, I'm the right age, in the right situation. Any one of her clients could have been me. If I'd had any sense.

Marilyn. The pain hits me in the stomach. I put a hand on the counter to steady myself. I never knew about any of this, I think, I never knew anything.

I see her tearful face in front of me. I want to hold her again, like only last Friday, last week maybe even to the minute, standing in her kitchen the day of the funeral. Her cheek on my shoulder, her curved ribs, I imagine, like a bird's. I would never have guessed she was so thin, so frail, wrapped tight as bandages.

For she seemed to me to be ever in a state of grief – her mother, her father, her patients. Some part of her own life missing, muffled almost by her surroundings. As I held her that morning, I thought, briefly, I should take you away from all this, I could take you away. But I didn't know where, and I didn't mean without me, like this, leaving me here.

And yet, I really don't know what I meant at all. Marilyn the strong one, Marilyn the one who knew most things about most things. And me, dizzy, a bit stupid. Why would she want me?

She wouldn't. I feel my breakfast churning again as I try not to see the other person who has it all together, so obviously and without me, and that's Suzanne.

My breakfast is coming back up. I lean over the sink. It's like my body doesn't want me to live, will only allow me rations, suffering. Like I shouldn't be alive.

Suzanne's face doesn't go away. It goes with me into the loo as I clean the bathroom, wash the floor. I sit down on the toilet, lid down. Jesus, my house has never been so clean as these last few days. I can't seem to do anything else.

I drop my head down and rub my hands, smelling of disinfectant and bleach, over my face. Why Suzanne, *Christ*.

When there are so many more people, people in the past who never seem to come back, who just sit there in their spaces, placid and immobile: Jane, the roommate I almost slept with after a night of drinking; Elizabeth the little girl I made strip and stand naked when I was ten; the boys down at the quarry who chased me away from their dirty magazine stash, most of whom I eventually fucked.

I raise my head. The answer's obvious, of course. Marilyn would laugh at me. Because I know these people, these things. They don't matter, not any more, and have no bearing on who I am now, the woman cleaning this loo.

But Suzanne, I noticed her when she arrived. Marilyn had disappeared somewhere; I was already a little worried about her. I remember feeling even then like a sort of guard dog, ever faithful. As if she couldn't protect herself.

Suzanne and Charles walked in. Doug immediately went to them, arms outstretched. He hugged Suzanne, and I saw her face over his shoulder, her eyes close, briefly. They stepped away from each other like they were doing a sort of dance, a court waltz, and Doug moved over to Charles. They had a hug, pat on the back exchange, and then they all stepped back, making an open circle.

And then I saw the glance that as far as I was concerned, gave the game away. Doug slid his eyes over to Suzanne, to her belly to be precise. It was an exposed look – no one was supposed to see, but I did. Suzanne looked down then and met his eyes, drew them back up to head level. There was an intimacy there, I'm sure of it. A look too complex for pleasantries, too full of good and bad, love and confusion. I knew then too, that Suzanne must be pregnant, even though she wasn't showing, not through her baggy clothes. And I knew that Doug, somehow, had something to do with it – by being the father, or not being the father, something. Their relationship, like a couple's, I could see from that one glance, was now changed forever, and they both knew it.

I remember that my concern for Marilyn increased to such an extent that my heart began to pound. I had to go find her quickly. I checked the kitchen once again and there was no sign of her. She must have gone upstairs, why, I couldn't imagine. I went to the stairs and started up them quickly – yes, there she was, coming toward me. With Adam next to her. She looked dazed, much as she'd looked since Tuesday. He looked – a little sulky, a little guilty. His standard expression.

They started down the steps and I reached out, took her hand. She clasped me like she was having trouble keeping her balance, and indeed, she was a little unsteady, her palm a little wet.

We moved along the hallway together, with Adam silently behind. Marilyn entered the sitting room and rushed over to Suzanne like she was embracing an old, close friend. I felt quite desperate for her – I had to tell her, but I couldn't.

Then Marilyn stepped back – "You're pregnant!" And Doug did his gruesome feigning of surprise, congratulations all around. I'd had enough by then – what a farce – and went to get Marilyn another drink. She looked...it was hard to say. She looked a bit lost. Suzanne, on the other hand, kept everyone spellbound. Yes, I'd had enough.

Fucking Suzanne. By the time I got back with Marilyn's drink she and Suzanne had collapsed onto the sofa. I could see Marilyn's hand resting on Suzanne's tummy, and I could also see Marilyn's naked desire for something Suzanne had, written all over her face. It was awful. She just seemed to disappear, even then. I should have known, I should have seen and stopped it. But I didn't. I was thinking about Suzanne, about how people like her always occupy more space than they deserve. Even now, sitting on the loo, staring at the shining tiles which I know will become immediately splashed and dirty – even now I wish I had just walked over, sat between them, and held onto

Marilyn's hand. Warmed it up, let it know something, anything. Instead of doing what I did, walk over to Charles, flirt with the boys, as always.

We have an early lunch of beans and fish fingers. They've been playing well all morning, the boys, and now Lewis in particular looks tired. Not surprising. Even Aaron, with his dark hair and slightly glowering face, looks subdued, cautious, I suppose.

I suggest a video. It's still drizzling outside, still unbearably hot and humid, like we're going round and round in the eye of some storm.

We move into the sitting room together. Lewis and Aaron go over to the video cabinet, puzzle over the choices with their backs to me, two such different children – dark hair, taller, rougher, and light hair, softer, reserved. But good for each other.

They turn as one and come over with their choice, *The Wizard of Oz*. Oh, I think, Dorothy disappears and tries and tries to get back to the people she loves. Not exactly appropriate. I look up to see the two of them settling on the sofa, Lewis' thumb already sneaking to his mouth. Or perhaps completely appropriate, I don't know.

I put it on. I don't know how to even raise the issue of Marilyn with them, especially if it means bringing it to the front of their minds, when it might be mercifully a little further away today. I've never been good with people, not good like Marilyn. I am aware that she would know just what to do. But I don't and never will, so there. So I must just go along for the ride, nipping and tucking and doing small repair jobs along the way, useless over the long haul.

The film starts. Within minutes, Dorothy's house lands with a thump in Oz, over the rainbow, and she opens the door to the world in Technicolor. The munchkins giggle, and sure enough, the magic bubble approaches, growing larger and larger, until pop! we see Glenda, the good witch. Her voice is pitched unnaturally high, and she has the slight look of Bette Davis, vampy. "Are you a good witch, or a bad witch?" she says. "Why, I'm not a witch at all," says Dorothy, "I'm Dorothy Gayle, from Kansas." The munchkins giggle again, raise their flowered heads briefly.

Poor Dorothy. Thrown into the middle of all this without any idea she's inadvertently making friends and enemies.

Glenda floats kitchily about the screen. Her eyebrows are permanently raised, and she does indeed look good, the epitome of good, like the white icing on a cake. And her voice – there's a familiarity to it, I can't place it. But I've heard it recently. It makes me feel...I don't know. It's double edged, somehow.

The boys, however, are completely entranced. I stand up, feeling I should do something if they're settled. Thankfully, just at that moment, the doorbell rings. I go to answer it.

There's a woman there holding a clipboard. My heart sinks, but then I notice she is heavily pregnant. Terrible, I remember that feeling. In the dead of summer, same as me with Aaron.

I let her start her spiel, something about a survey to do with baby products, nappies or something. She sways a little, or at least I think she does. "Of course," I say, "why don't you come in for a minute?" She smiles gratefully, and we go through to the kitchen. Next door I can hear the munchkins singing about the dead witch. I pop my head in and both boys are still engrossed.

"Right," I say, pulling out a chair. "Take some weight off that bump." She laughs a little. "Can I get you something to drink?" She nods.

I pour us both an orange juice and tonic water, remembering how appealing tart things were when I was pregnant. I sit down across from her. She is older than I first thought, about my age.

"First one?" I say, indicating the bump.

"Oh, no." She shakes her head. "Third. And last. A bit unexpected." She laughs a little again, sounding puffed still. "It seems harder this time." She stretches her feet out in front of her – they are red and swollen at the top of her shoes – and laces her fingers over her belly. Her fingers too are swollen, expanding over her rings. She reaches forward for her glass. "Thanks," she says, takes a long drink.

Her hair is partly stuck to her face and forehead; the rest weaves in wisps around her. She smiles at me, looking me in the eye. I am struck by something, but I'm not sure what. It's just that everything seems familiar today, one long déjà vu. From next door, the scarecrow's song drifts out like some kind of maudlin commentary: "I would not be such a nuthin, my head all full of stuffin, my heart all full of pain..."

"Yours next door?" The woman suddenly says.

"Just one of them."

"Ah," she smiles. "More on the way?"

"I don't think so," I say. "The other belongs to a friend of mine, she – " I see the woman's eyebrows rise and look behind me just in time. Lewis is standing there.

"Hilary?" His voice is quavery. Then he starts crying. I reach for him and pull him onto my lap. He feels thin to Aaron's sturdiness. He lets out a big sigh and lets his head fall on my shoulder.

I look around his head to the woman. She looks back at us, her face full of sympathy. She finishes her drink and glances down at her watch. She touches it and mouths at me, "Must be going."

"Right," I mouth back. I loosen my thumb and point it up, "okay."

As soon as she stands up I can see she needs a loo. I point out the door. "Through the kitchen," I say, quietly. She nods and disappears.

Lewis sits up as soon as she's gone. He looks completely awful, red eyes, purple shadows underneath, his nose running into his mouth.

I don't know what to say to him. Dorothy and the scarecrow are saving the tin man now, the one who keeps crying and crying, always on the verge of rusting himself up forever.

I hear the toilet flush. Dorothy trying to get back home – I've always found it terrible. Poor Lewis. I wonder if Marilyn would reprimand me for showing it to him at all. But you never know how kids are going to take things, what goes in, what goes over their heads or around them, arrows that strike the heart or nothing at all.

The woman emerges. "Thanks," she says, and she does look more comfortable. I start to struggle up but she holds up a hand: don't worry. I smile.

In a few seconds, I hear the door close. We never even did the survey.

Lewis has recovered himself to some extent, although I can't imagine how. He has, unnervingly, Marilyn's inscrutability about him, almost a passivity. Which makes him difficult to comfort.

He places the tips of his fingers gently on my chest, studies them.

"She's not coming back, is she?" he says. "Dad says that she might be back any time, any second he said last night, but I know that's not true."

I can't say anything. He begins to cry again, gently this time, the tears rolling down his face with every blink. "People don't do that, do they? They don't just go away and come back. When you die, you die, that's it. You're gone. Mom told me. Dad told me too, but Mom told me first." He glances at me, his eyes cautious under the quick lids. "Grandad died. And he's not coming back."

"No, that's right." I want to squeeze all of this out of him, but I can't. "Your grandad is dead now. But your mum —"

I am aware that I am even using the wrong word for Marilyn, how unfair can it be on him, that no one he knows except Doug can even say her name correctly. "Your mother – we're not sure what's happened to her – she might be lost, she might be thinking..."

He shakes his head violently. "No! That's what Dad says, but he's wrong. She wouldn't, she wouldn't do it. She would call me, she always calls me." Suddenly he struggles down off my lap. He is red now, angry. "You don't know anything!" he screams at the top of his voice, and runs, bumping into things, out of the room and up the stairs. I hear a door slam, and sobbing coming from Aaron's room.

Christ. I put my head down, close my eyes and find that I'm crying too. He's right, I don't know anything, I can't help him at all. Hell, I can't even help myself. The problem is, I was beginning to love her, and as soon as I think this that clearly, the truth of it is embarrassing. I run over the checklist in my mind: thinking about her obsessively, dreaming about her, longing for her. Somehow. For something I've never even experienced. How ridiculous, how foolish, to move closer and closer to something which doesn't exist, or which dissolves if I get too close. But then again, that's the story of my life.

I squeeze my eyes, forcing the last tears out. Now is not the time or the place. There's Lewis to think about.

When I raise my head, Aaron is standing silently on the other side of the table. "Mum?" he says, when he sees I'm looking. For an instant I wonder how often he wants to say something, but doesn't, because no one is paying any attention.

"Yes darling," I say.

"What's happened?"

"Lewis's just upset, sweetheart. About Marilyn not being around. It's just upsetting for him. For all of us," I add.

He nods, trying to understand.

"Like you would be upset if you didn't know where I was."

"Like that time I got lost in *Marks and Spencers*," he says.

"Yes, sort of."

"But you found me," he says. "Are you going to find Marilyn?"

I hug him tightly. I can feel my eyes filling up again. "I hope so."

I settle Aaron back in front of the *Wizard of Oz* with a snack, and go to wash my face before going to Lewis. He can't see me like this; I need to be strong for him, unflappable. Over the sink, I reach for my watch to take it off. It's not there, I must have taken it off earlier. I look where I always put it, on the shelf above the sink. It's not there either. As I feel my stomach contract – I've lost one of the nicest things I own – I know immediately and with certainty that the pregnant woman has stolen it.

This is ridiculous, I think. What is the world coming to. We could have been friends – would have been friends, given more time. Or not. Who am I fooling? Only myself as usual. People steal when the opportunity presents, for lots of reasons. A conversation hardly stands in the way of money, of something you want. And, to top it off, she knows I won't report it, that I perhaps felt just sorry enough for her, and she's right. All I can think is I hope she was desperate, then realise she probably was. It's not even like she needs one for herself; I remember the one on her wrist – white, with black numbering. Perfectly serviceable. She just took mine because it was there, because it was waiting to happen, irresistibly shining just above where she no doubt washed her hands, looked at her own face. Nothing wrong with her face, I think, but we don't tend to like the one we have.

I push the incident out of my mind. There are more important things. I go to Lewis, but he's asleep, the best thing.

He looks angelic, his thumb hanging just outside his lips, curled up. I cover him with Aaron's sheet, and go back downstairs.

Aaron is quiet on the sofa, caught up in the film once more. It's the part where Dorothy is trapped in the wicked witch's castle, with the hourglass and the crystal ball. Suddenly Auntie Em materialises in the ball, and begins calling for Dorothy, plaintively, almost angrily: *Dorothy! Dorothy! We're all worried about you.* And Dorothy calls too, *Auntie Em, Auntie Em,* but of course no one hears her. She can see and hear her old life, but no one knows anything about her now, if she's even alright. Auntie Em appears in the ball in black and white, like an old photograph. Dorothy, with her red lips and shoes, blue dress, is past that now, and for some reason it's too late. But I always start crying at that bit, and this afternoon is no exception. It's the whole idea that she can't get back, she never really gets back, and that even at the end, when she does click her heels and return – and it's all a bad dream – even then, no one believes her. No one believes she was ever anyone or anyplace different. The end always makes me cry as well, but for opposite reasons, because in the long run I fall for it: I'm glad she's home, whatever shape she's in, and whatever she's left behind.

I lie in the bath that night and think, the end of another terrible day. Doug was very late picking Lewis up, and I didn't like to think why. Poor Lewis. He's right – it's like she's dead already – tragically young. 'Young Mum' – I can see the tabloids – 'Disappeared'. It's like magic, over the rainbow indeed. When I was young I really used to believe that, that it was possible to just – whoosh, disappear into so-called thin air. As I got older, the thin air became another world which existed in parallel to this one: through the wardrobe, the magic side of life. The other side of the rainbow. And it was always good, it was a good thing when you went.

The flip side of this belief is that I used to spend a lot of time waiting. Waiting to disappear myself, without warning. Or waiting for someone to come back, sweep me off of my feet. It was only when I met Adam that I felt I'd stopped waiting. He being what, or whom, I was waiting for.

We met at a party. Of course, this would be the case. Good money goes on Marilyn and Doug meeting in a seminar, in the library, something. But Adam and me, a party. I'd gone with a girlfriend of mine. She was stunning, with a lovely figure. Long medium brown hair, big brown eyes. Tits and legs that didn't stop. Katherine, she was called. She was beautiful, but she was also largely unaware of it, the extent of it anyway, and this made her fun to be around. She was funny, sardonic, and made me feel more attractive. Almost like we were the couple.

At this party we were standing in the corner just looking, and over came Adam with someone else – Jim, I now remember. Adam went for Katherine – typical – and Jim and I were resigned to each other. The four of us spent the whole evening together, and later, a little worse for wear, I seem to remember screwing Jim in his car. I don't know where Katherine and Adam were, but Jim was a good lay, despite his unprepossessing – in fact, downright unappealing – exterior. A bit like me, probably. Unattractive but sexy in an experienced way. There weren't fireworks, and he was shorter, more awkward than I usually go for – but he knew what to do, which even then made a nice change.

Ah, Jim. Those were the days. I had a string of them, it was exciting. I used to sit on the Tube with my legs apart, waiting for one to bite. It never took long.

As it turned out, Katherine had rejected Adam's advances that first night. Girls being girls, I knew the truth of the matter within hours, though I didn't let on to Adam until after we were married. His rendition of the evening was kinder to his pride: she wasn't his type, all along he was thinking of me, etc. All complete bollocks, of course, and again true to type. His great fault always has been and always will be his utter predictability.

So why did I marry him? Fuck knows.

I slide back up to sitting in the bath and reach for my wine. The water's getting cold. I know I married him partly because I was flattered, because he seemed to need me, partly because he was the best looking and potentially the most successful man I'd ever dated. Who knows the rest of it. The truth is, until recently, I'd expected more, more of everything. And I can trace that feeling back to expecting more of him, of us together. But we never made much more than half a go of it. God knows why he married me. Probably because I was good in bed. And because he never knew what I was going to do next.

To my mild surprise, he isn't home by the time I'm out of the bath and started dinner, nor does he phone. Bastard. You would think I was used to it after all these years and to some extent I am. But all that thought about how we first met, and his rather luscious eyes, his early declarations, has made me want to see him.

I keep dinner in the oven. I sit and watch television, an evening soap, thinking about how my life has become one, at least for a while. I can smell the dinner, not exciting, but a new recipe – I can smell it burning, the potatoes curling at the edges.

In a minute I will go turn it off and leave it in there, so it is as hard as a rock by the time he comes home.

My own stomach rumbles from hunger, but I know I won't eat. Vindictive, yes – and I feel what must be a rather horrible smile cover my face, I actually feel my lips stretch out. He'll just feel that much worse when he does come home, it's that simple.

Really, most of me couldn't give a shit. It's just the generalised, and I think pathetic, feeling that life wasn't supposed to be like this. How typical that sounds, textbook even: whatever exists or used to exist between Adam and me wasn't supposed to just drain away, like it sprung a slow leak, a hairline fracture, to use his terms, through which everything seeped, imperceptibly, silently, away.

Now Marilyn, she would be different. But as soon as I think it, I steer my mind away. Who am I kidding? She was happily married, more than I am anyway. Married to Doug, the happily married man.

I stand up too fast and the blood rushes from my head. What a mess. I rest my head against the French door frame to steady myself. It's nine-thirty and not even dark yet, the sky almost a sea blue. There's something spooky about a never-ending day, perhaps because we know that the balance of that is a never-ending night in the dead of winter. It's just – not natural.

Tears again rise to the surface. I'm fed up with them. How long will I cry for her, for heaven's sake? Will she be back by winter? Or never.

What am I even talking about. I look at my life, I look at the way I feel about her, or think I feel, and it's obvious. But surely there must be more to this than escape, than change. I can hardly bear to consider the trashy clichés: women know each other better than men do, men will always let us down. But how do I even know these things? I have no idea what's true, what I believe or the path I want to follow, any more. If there's one thing you can say for Marilyn and me, for who she is to me, it's this: she has shaken up everything I thought I knew, so different from anyone or anything I thought I loved.

I can feel the anger now, so close to exploding these last few days, boiling again. I carry my empty wine glass, fearful of my hand unconsciously contracting, crushing it, back into the kitchen. I am not even in the position to consider anything objectively, I think. To consider love. Before now, I had never even thought that any other love, other than the one you know, the one you think you've chosen, was possible. That I was capable of any other love. But now I think I know differently, and she's gone. And I just watched her go.

I find myself mostly drunk, tears running down my face, feeling my way blindly through them upstairs into the spare room. I really have had enough of this, I think. If nobody will save me, then, well. I kneel down, and pull the suitcase out. I unzip it – as I suspected, musty. So long since we've gone anywhere, no wonder. I fold the top all the way back and slip it under the bed. It needs a good airing.

I make my way to our bedroom. I will fall asleep quickly, and may even be lucky enough to have a good few hours before the dreams start. I am comforted as I drift off by the thought that I am going over to Marilyn's tomorrow, to help Doug do some laundry, sift through some of her things again. And by the thought of the suitcase. I know I will be able to smell her again, at least. When you come to something fresh, it's always stronger.

Tuesday

Marilyn is standing there crying. We are in her kitchen. Her head is down in her hands, her hair falling forward. I go to her, wrap my arms around her. She smells – sweet, clean. Like she just washed her hair this morning. Even as I hold her, I imagine her in the shower, combing her fingers through the length, leaning her head back, alone. And then she smells of heat, like she has just stepped out of the sun, sun in the morning.

She rests her head on my shoulder, and one hand reaches for the top of my arm, which she squeezes, hard. She is still crying, and I feel the tears soak through my cotton shirt. I say, "I'm sorry," several times, knowing nothing about what she's feeling, except perhaps something I can't remember. I hold her so tightly she must be bruising. She, who is so sensible, so plain and loving, relaxes into me. "What am I going to do?" she says.

I don't know what we're doing. Where everything was spinning around, now together we seem to be in the eye of the storm. It is silent. My heart beats so hard I think she can hear it. I pull back and look at her, up slightly as she's taller. I wonder, can she feel the earth turning, throwing us together? There is no choice but to go in; there's nothing outward, out there for us. Anyway the wind is increasing, blowing us more strongly together. And finally she smells of flowers, strong, almost musty. But beautiful.

She meets my eyes. We kiss. Her lips are shockingly soft, I can't believe it. I can't get hold of them, they slip around, loose. I am aware that my lips must be the same to her, soft against soft, softer than anything. We push together, pushing for something central, something to hold onto.

Even before I am completely awake I am aware of two things: that it is another sweltering morning, and that Adam is still snoring gently beside me.

The dream drifts around, the feel of her. Something about the heat, I don't know – I'm dreaming of her every night.

Adam trips over his own snore and moves a little. I wonder what he's dreaming about. I feel as though I am on fire, all the points of me flashing, love coming out of my skin, evaporating uselessly. I imagine all the unused love, floating around overhead like clouds, angels, dead people.

I want to be dead if she's dead.

Immediately I think, no that's not true, I don't. I can't believe I've thought that. Leftovers of a dream only she would be able to analyse. I swing my legs out of bed and sit up. I miss her, it's as simple as that. I miss – nothing really. Some idea I had of the future. Yet it's really of my life before now as well, before Adam and Aaron, back to school days.

I stand up, go to the bathroom and wash. I raise my head and look at my wet face in the mirror. The water running down my face looks like tears. I think, what would I do if she came back today? My heart leaps at the thought, I imagine the scene: I go to the door, open it, and there she is, she says, "I've come back for you, come with me, I don't know what I was thinking."

I dry my face. Of course she does, I think, yeah right. That's really something she would do.

When I turn, Aaron is in the doorway. His hair is mussed from sleep and his eyes are extra wide. "Morning, darling," I say. "Sleep well?" He nods, then says, "I had a dream that Marilyn came back."

I go over to him and crouch down, hold his hands. "That's nice, darling, that's a nice dream."

He shakes his head. "No, it wasn't really. She was weird, she was a bit...scary. I ran away."

I pull him to me. He's too newly awake to be thinking much of anything, and he soon extracts himself, wanders back to his room.

After he leaves, I go back into the bedroom and start to get dressed. Scary, he said. I suppose when anyone comes back, no matter how much you love them, they're always a stranger.

I remember, as I stand at the kitchen sink doing the washing up, that two weeks ago today, at about the same time, Marilyn was doing the same thing. Breakfast dishes. The day her father died. The smallest things become at once absurd and of great import. I wonder what she thinks about it now. If she can think anything.

Or perhaps she wasn't doing the dishes at all, but I just thought she was from my vantage point, coming down the path. Perhaps she was staring out the window, in a daze, premonition-like.

Premonitions do not run in my family, and if we ever think we have one, like Aaron appeared to this morning, they are never right. I wish, in fact, that I did have them, then I might feel I knew something, more than this moment, and the next when it happens, and the next. It's not good enough, not knowing what's going to happen. I used to love the thrill of it, the big blank day and night, waiting. Looking at it now, I'm amazed I'm not in more pieces, the way I used to throw myself around, desperate to make an imprint, to make something out of life.

But now, well. Of course that morning we can be pretty sure Marilyn wasn't pondering anything so deep. People don't usually, thank goodness. She was probably wondering what to have for dinner, what to do tonight, something about sex in there somewhere, there normally is. God knows. I don't even remember what I was thinking – did I love her then? No, not really. I felt drawn to her, but as a friend. She was well travelled, interesting, smart. Worldly. And there's the children.

She received the phone call, though, and everything changed. I can hardly bear to think of it. Her face, everything left it, everything I had ever seen as Marilyn. And in its place, she became something, someone else, completely emptied, waiting to be filled.

She wasn't even really looking at me, but I felt something in me rush through, the need to pour myself into her, fill her up again, give her what she wants. Wanted.

Can it be that difficult? Can it be that wrong? I saw a space and filled it, and unexpectedly, inexplicably, she too rushed in like water, and filled me. It was, really, a surprising bonus.

But now. I shake my pruned-up hands free of the soapy water and dry them, put the kettle on. Now the time I would count without her has already eclipsed the time with her. We spoke every day for less than a week – yet I know, I am certain, that she is one of the great loves of my life.

And the proof, as if I needed any, is that I long for her with every bone and muscle in my body, every nerve and tip of me. If I think about it, I can still feel my nipples and groin flashing, like a pinball machine, flayed.

On the other hand, I think as I sit down with tea, this is completely, utterly ridiculous, absurd. On cue, Aaron comes in, wondering where Lewis is.

"He's spending the day with his father," I say. "But they'll be over later. I'm making dinner for everyone."

"Oh," he says, and goes out again. I have no idea what he's thinking. I never, ever, know what's really going on with him anymore, except for first thing in the morning or last thing at night. Like his father.

That afternoon in the garden, I get itchy feet. I can feel them, literally tickling me underneath, hot and twitching.

I need to go somewhere, but my car's in the garage, Adam has the other. And Doug and Lewis will be over soon, it feels too soon. It's the end of another hot dusty day, although at least the rain has stopped. It feels like the end of summer, like everything's dying.

Aaron plays on his bicycle, whizzing up and down the path. I go over to the shady part of the garden, in the cool, and bend down, half prepared to weed although it's not really my scene. In the place of going, I guess doing will have to suffice. The hostas, water loving and luscious looking, are failing, in spite of the rain. As are the lilies I can see behind them, bitten and rotted. Their flowers began to show, then became sidetracked with water, damp. Everywhere I look things are dying.

I feel something like panic rising up in me and I don't know why. Again I think I might throw up. I force myself to go on, to go past it, and place my fingers in the dirt. I scrabble around, feeling sicker and sicker, and finally find what I know will be there somewhere from the number of ants swarming: a dead bird, only the inedible bits left, bones and a few feathers, some guts, frozen in time like the fossils you hear about. An array of flies, earwigs and the ants climb over and through it. I retch. Too bad anything it might reveal about us will come too late, after we are all dead and buried, when none of it matters, when nothing can be done.

I stand up and go inside, feeling dizzy. No wonder I hate gardening, I think. It's dirty, disgusting and depressing. Everything dies, gets diseased. I look at myself in the hall mirror. I look like shit, like I haven't seen the sun in years, my hair clamped into a tail of fur in the back. Ears sticking out, almost black eyes. Slight moustache, red enough lips that turn down at the corners.

I feel it happening again, and manage to get myself into the bathroom before it comes. As I throw up I begin to cry, and the combination of the retching and sobbing strikes me even now as absurd, so that if I had room in my lungs I know I would be laughing too. But I haven't and I'm not, and in that state I hear Aaron come in, walk up to the door: "Mum? Mu-um! I need the loo!"

I am finished anyway. As I walk out he doesn't even glance up, but rushes in and slams the door. As children do, I think, remember it's what children do.

I go into the kitchen. A much better idea. Everything is waiting for me there, dinner for Aaron and Lewis, dinner for the three of us.

I start chopping for the soup, a gazpacho I'm already looking forward to eating. There's an odd precision to this, much better than messy gardening. As I go through the tomatoes and peppers, I let myself relax into it. I begin to feel better. Aaron has semi-followed me in, as he usually does; I can hear him dump out his train track next door, already able to while away the hours, waiting for Lewis.

I half-cook pasta for the boys and for us. It's the one thing I know I'm good at – well, the second, the first being sex of course. I'm certainly better at cooking than Marilyn was: I remember the meal I had at hers that last night, the dull pasta and lettuce leaves.

Marilyn was not a good cook. I think this, throwing some salt over my left shoulder, and wonder at the past tense. Lewis thinks she's dead – is she? I think of her in the past even if she isn't, I think of her as gone – like anytime anyone or any place leaves you, that old fashioned feudal saying, "so and so is dead to me!"

Also, to cut someone dead. Stop everything, even though the heart is still ticking, like my heart is, like the tin man who doesn't even know he has one until the end.

And too, how can I think badly of her at all? 'Death' and 'bad person' seem to go in opposite directions from each other, yet must co-exist. I don't understand, but do. I think about my own mother, my own father, how I will feel when they die. No one's perfect. She wasn't perfect. There I go again, I think, *was*. I can hardly bring myself to get to the end of the thought, but it flies off of its own accord, speaking as it goes: she wasn't perfect. But I loved her.

Doug and Lewis arrive at six. Lewis looks even paler than usual, the strain showing, purple shadows under his eyes. Typically, he is polite to a fault, but he doesn't meet my eyes, or rise to Aaron's chatter about what they can do after they eat. My heart goes out to both of them – Aaron trying so hard, Lewis struggling – but I can't do anything about it, and eventually they go, Lewis trailing behind, upstairs to play.

Doug is quiet too, to an extent unusual even for him, the bear-like man who keeps his opinions to himself. He seems...almost angry, and I wonder if it is at me. Then again, he has every right to be angry. At anyone he wants.

The boys are in their pyjamas by the time Adam comes home at nearly seven thirty. Doug and Adam, too, barely speak, each guarding something, I think, I wonder. I make excuses and go to the loo, look at myself in the mirror again. I get up close, as close as I can and still be in focus. I wonder if I too am hiding something, have something to hide. Or if I am giving it all away.

Back in the kitchen they are both laying the table, moving for all the world like two old women around it. Eventually, we sit down to eat.

I find, as I dish the soup, that I can't stop wondering when we were last all together. Surely not that night, surely not. But I think back – yes, it is, it is that night. Then – then there is a horrible synchronicity to this. Then Aaron might be right after all, she will walk right in, looking like – what? The dead bird comes into my mind. Risen from the dead.

Oh my god. I sit down. The other two still seem antsy, unsettled; neither can meet my eye or each other's. Like me, earlier in the garden. The heat.

I say, "Please start." We all set to it, lift the spoons to our mouths and swallow. Doug and I begin to speak at once. "No, you" he says, and I say, "I was only going to comment on the weather. What heat! I felt like I was going to jump out of my skin today."

They both nod. "Yes, terrible," says Doug, "and the smell —" He stops. "The last of Marilyn's father's flowers are going, and everywhere —" He stops again. "Everywhere I go in the house I can smell them rotting." He takes another spoonful, swallows. "For some reason I can't bring myself to throw them away."

My chest contracts with guilt. I was over there helping him straighten up, only Saturday. "I'm sorry, Doug," I say, "I should have thought. I should have cleared them out for you..."

He holds his hand up to stop me. "No," he says, "you've already done so much. It's just me being silly. I need to press on, do it myself. Marilyn would have."

"Yes." Adam speaks for the first time. "She would have, through thick and thin, wouldn't she." He scrapes out his bowl. "All of which makes me think she's going to be okay, you know." He glances sideways at Doug, who continues to eat his soup, head down. "She's strong, in a quiet way. Resilient. Even at the hospital, when I saw her that morning, she wouldn't get upset, not really upset. She was still thinking, wondering what to do next." He folds up his napkin, and places it on the table. I hate it when he does that, before everyone else is done. "She has what I think they call an inner strength. It should serve her well."

No one says anything. I'm thinking, I didn't know they saw each other at the hospital, no one ever mentioned they'd seen each other at the hospital. I'm also thinking, why doesn't he feel foolish, telling Doug and me something that is so obvious, something we know about her already, like he's telling us something new, that only he is privy to. Typical.

"You never told me you saw her at the hospital," I say, and it comes out a bit sharper than I intended.

"What?" he says, casually.

"You never told me. That you saw her there."

His face immediately closes over, and he doesn't even have to say what he is thinking, that no matter what he says now I won't believe him. Which is probably true.

Doug, in an uncharacteristically warm gesture, places his hand over mine on the table. "The day her dad died, Hilary. At the hospice. I was there too."

The addition of his last sentence, with all of its implications, drops into the middle of the table like a ball no one wants to catch.

I collect the bowls. "Oh, I see," I manage, and bring them over to the counter.

After the meal is over — it was good, after all, and I feel almost cheerful — we all go through to the sitting room, where Aaron's train track unfortunately still crisscrosses the room. We are all well oiled, and negotiate our way around it with difficulty, collapse into the soft sofa and chair.

"I can't stand the sight of this thing," Adam says, and makes a move to stand.

"No, don't," I say. "He'll be upset; he likes things to be there in the morning."

Adam holds his hands out. "For God's sake, Hilary. Look at this. You're too easy on him." He flops down again.

What's his problem, I think. He's being a prat. Maybe he wishes I were Marilyn, then I might keep the house neat.

Adam turns away from my silence and toward Doug. "So," he says, his voice deliberately calmed, "Is there any news?"

Doug leans forward in his chair. He shoots me a look I don't understand. "Not news, exactly — but we think some of her things are missing..."

"What, a week later?" Adam interrupts. "You would think this would have been discovered days ago. Jesus. It's outrageous!"

"No, well, see that's the thing. No one's sure, hell, I'm not even sure, but it seems like the things that are missing now, weren't missing before. That's why it's so weird."

"Oh," says Adam, looking perplexed.

I feel the same old panic mounting in me, the stiffness in my neck. I can't turn my head to look at anyone. "How strange," I say. "What do they think has happened?"

"Well..."

"Like what, she watched the house and then came back in when you and Lewis were out?" says Adam.

"Something like that," Doug says. He puts his head in his hands. "It just sounds ridiculous. It just doesn't make sense."

"That doesn't sound like Marilyn," I say.

Doug looks up. "No, exactly, that's what I told them. She just wouldn't do it, she just wouldn't. If she needed something she would buy something new; she's got cards. She wouldn't sneak around. Anyway, the things that seem to be missing..."

"What are they?" says Adam.

"Weird things, strange things. Like −" he leans forward, almost conspiratorially. I realise that he's quite drunk. "Like socks. I ask you, socks. This time of year! And one of her silk scarves. There's a space on one of the hooks. For the life of me I can't even remember if all the hooks were even being used, that's what's so silly. But there are two doubled up, and they think that's because there wasn't room. And," he says, spreading his hands, "to add insult to injury, I can't even remember all of her scarves, I don't know them off by heart. And they're asking me all these questions..." He sighs. "Fuck knows."

I stand up and slip around the track over to Doug. I perch on the arm of the chair, and put my hand on his shoulder. "You poor thing," I say, "this is so difficult."

Adam shifts in his seat. "Presumably," he says, "they haven't been used."

"What?" says Doug.

"The cards."

Doug shakes his head. "Nope. Not even the cash card."

My bum hurts from sitting on the chair. I stand up and move Adam over on the sofa.

Doug sits back and finishes his drink. "The strangest thing about it is," he continues, "I feel almost angry that there's been some change, like if you're going to go, *go* – but if you're not..."

"Come back," I finish.

"Exactly," Doug says.

"The thing is," I say, almost without thinking. "What's she coming back to?"

The effect is quite dramatic; both men practically swing their bodies to face me full on. Behind Doug's head I can see the summer evening, again heavy with heat and rain. I see the street lamps on, bright yellow against the yellow sky. I think, this time two weeks ago I was bending down to Marilyn's front step, placing the lilies there, turning away. I was standing at the bottom of the path, looking at her stare out the window, not noticing me. Her face was blank, lonely.

Finally, Doug says, "What are you saying?"

I pause only for a second before replying. I know what I am going to say is true, but I'm not sure saying it will do any good, for Marilyn anyway.

"I'm saying that at the end there Marilyn didn't seem very happy."

"Oh for god's sake!" snorts Adam. Doug doesn't say anything.

I can feel myself starting to tremble all over – I recognise it as fear or anger, anything too powerful hold in. And once, with Marilyn, I remember now, it was lust.

"What did she say to you?" Doug says now, quietly.

"Well, nothing really." I know I'm trying to cover my tracks now, but I also know it's useless and what will come out will come out. "She didn't say anything. It's just that that night you were late."

"We've been over this," Doug says shortly.

"Yes, but what you may not know is that she'd planned a special dinner, she'd agreed to send Lewis over to us..."

Adam stands up and heads into the kitchen. "That's not enough, Hilary," he says, "a little disappointment –" He goes in, reappears with water. "Her father had just died, only days before. Surely she had more pressing things on her mind." He turns to Doug. "I would have thought something about that would be far more likely...nothing you were aware of?"

Doug waves his hands. "The police asked me all about that. I told them she never mentioned anything that might be bothering her about her dad dying, no more than the usual..." He turns to me. "Presumably they asked you as well?" I nod. They had, they had asked me things for hours it seems, but it must have served its purpose, because they hadn't been back since.

"She never mentioned anything to me, either," I say. "She talked about other things, like wanting another child." I stop, then start. "Wanting to spend more time with Doug."

Doug sits back. "She didn't want another child," he says, with finality. "We discussed it many times. In fact, she was dead set against it."

Are all men prats, I think, or just the ones I know? It's as if he never knew her. "I'm sorry, Doug," I say, "that's not the impression I had." I glance at Adam, who is glaring at me, but I don't care. "Seeing Suzanne at the funeral practically did her in."

Doug looks increasingly confused and hot.

"She couldn't tell you, of course," I go on, warming to my theme now. I stand up, go over to the shelf for some chocolate. "I'm not sure she could tell you much of anything, to be truthful, anything important. I know you two supposedly had this solid relationship –"

"That's enough, Hilary," says Adam. "It's none of our business."

I hear myself laugh, and the sound is, even to my own ears, a little nasty. "It bloody well is," I say, "if it isn't ours, whose business is it?"

"Right," says Adam, tolerantly, as if I am mad. He looks at Doug meaningfully.

This makes me furious. "Don't you start that!" I say. "No wonder she had to get out, you two are just the most ridiculous pieces of work." I can feel I'm going to cry soon if I'm not careful, so I rush on. "You just don't see, do you? One by one she lost everyone she ever loved, including you Doug —"

"Now hang on," he interrupts, then looks at Adam.

"You don't have anything to say to that, do you," I go on, "because you know it's true, what with you and Suzanne carrying on." Doug jumps to his feet, and makes a move toward me. I hold up my hand, and, amazingly, he stops. "You forget, I spoke to Charles at the wake." Doug shifts. "And I'm more than a little perceptive about these things."

Adam walks over now and joins Doug. Both of them are standing a meter away from me, just waiting. For what, I wonder. For me to transgress to the point where they will have to 'deal with' me? Like they 'dealt with' Marilyn...?

I feel her close to me now, as I go on. I feel her strength, her hopes and sadness over having to leave. I feel almost *inhabited* by her, in fact, and realise even as I stand there that that's what love does, it shifts the souls of two people so they are closer together, overlapping in places. So I know what I am saying is right, it has her blessing.

I feel calmer now, and can speak normally. I look straight at Doug. "She had to get out, Doug, she had to escape. Her life had been —" I think about what it was, what it wasn't. In truth, I could see from here, it was rather like mine. "– an immense disappointment."

Doug is calmer now too. "And what about Lewis," he says, coldly. "She wouldn't leave him. She was a wonderful mother."

"Perhaps that's just the point," I say, equally as coldly, bolstered by the feeling of Marilyn being close. "Perhaps that just wasn't good enough. Sometimes we have to lose even the people we love the most, we have to leave them."

Adam reaches out and takes my arm, leads me by the elbow back to a chair. I don't want to be in the room, and resolve not to be for long. As soon as a gap appears, I will make a break for it.

Doug, too, turns and sits back down. Adam remains standing. "This is all," Adam starts, "very difficult for everyone, can we at least acknowledge that?" He takes a deep breath. "We all loved her, that was the thing about her. It's like, we didn't know it at the time..." He stops again. I think, he has a real gift for stating the obvious; somebody needs to shut him up. Then I think, he's right, we all loved her, even him in his own way, even though he probably thought he just wanted a shag.

"Don't you see?" he goes on. "We're grieving, that's all. There's a hole right in the middle of us, the middle of Lewis and

Aaron too, the middle of this room – right there where the train tracks circle. The space in the centre everyone just rides around. But it's there. Hell –" He laughs a little, and runs his hand through his hair. "I know I hardly knew her. But I just – miss her like hell."

Suddenly, I notice Doug is crying. It's not a very manly crying, sobbing or anything, it's a tears-trickling-down kind of crying, and he doesn't wipe his face, he just stares straight ahead.

Then he speaks. "That was very moving Adam, bravo." I am momentarily confused. But when he next talks, his voice is ragged, furious. "Too bad you guys don't know what the hell you're talking about. Neither of you do." He looks at each of us in turn. "Up until now I've let everything slide. You've been kind to us, especially Lewis, and I know Marilyn was grateful to you after her father died. And I'm even willing to accept that you might know some things about Marilyn I don't know. But that's as far as it goes. In fact, you don't know her at all, really know her. And you don't love her, you can't love her, like I do..." He breaks down, and puts his head in his hands.

I can't stand it anymore. I get to my feet, and, without a word, leave the room. No one stops me.

I pause at the top of the stairs, but Adam and Doug are silent. Typical.

I pass along the corridor, stop and look in on the boys. Aaron is sleeping with his back to the door. Lewis, though, is lying on his back, one arm flung off the edge of the bed. Then, as I take another step, his eyes open shutter-like. They stare at me blindly, and I freeze, caught in headlights, although he looks the more frightened. Then, just as suddenly, he closes them again. Spooky when that happens, I think, like someone else is in there. I move forward carefully, shake the covers over both of them, back out of the room.

I go into the spare room and lie down on the bed. It's not a very comfortable bed; I can feel the springs coming up through it. In fact, the room itself isn't very comfortable, decorated with all the things and made up with all the sheets which we deemed to be below par. Nevertheless, it is comforting to look up at the white ceiling, away from Doug and Adam, away from my own bedroom, the marital bed. The ceiling warps slightly as I look. Adam's right for once, I think, this is all a bit much. We are all drunk, drunk and in pain.

I close my eyes and the spinning gets worse. Then, to my relief, I feel Marilyn again, somehow inside me. I can even glance at her face, half-hidden as she bends over to cry, like in my dream. Strange how as soon as someone is gone, it's the first thing to go from the memory. You would think it would be the last. The expression, the eyes.

As I lie there, I know with nauseating certainty that she will never be back. None of us, after all, are worth saving, worth coming back for. Except poor Lewis, and he's her unwitting sacrifice. In any situation, there's always someone left behind, someone you wish you didn't have to leave. And that person spends whatever time remaining trying to fill the empty space. It's the way of the world, losing something, being the one lost. We've all been there, or will be soon.

Shit. I sit up. Whatever I could have been to her, I never will be now. We are all just incidentals, breakages occurring in the normal course of living, all just caught in her wake, the impression she left on the world, her own small thumb print. We will peel away from her like skiers over water, let go the rope and ride to shore, somehow. Except Lewis. He will be dragged on a long time, I can see this, practically drowning, the tow gone all wrong.

Bloody woman. I'm not sure who I'm talking to now, me or Marilyn. But I know that the more I try to shake myself free, the more I want her. Uselessly, stupidly.

I stand up and go over to the mirror. What is the real reason she had to go? I thought it was because of Doug, because of Suzanne, and maybe Adam. And yes, though I wouldn't admit it downstairs, maybe because of her dad, because she was the only one left. Certainly she'd had enough of losing, but the same could be said of all us. Especially now.

I look at my eyes. Something occurs to me that hadn't before. Maybe it was me. Maybe there was simply no other reason but me, what I said, who I was, who I might be. Maybe she was perfectly happy until I came along.

I back up and sit down again on the bed. And yet. And yet once something is known it cannot be gone back on, it can't be taken back. It's like it was waiting to happen; surprising as it is, it was waiting to happen. She can't blame me for that.

I close my eyes again, trying to concentrate, to feel her. And, on cue, she comes up, happy Marilyn, knowing Marilyn, welcoming Marilyn. Not the one who's scared, unsure, angry. But the one I love, the one who might, just might, love me. Yes, there she is. And, what's this? Yes, she's celebrating. She doing a kind of joyful hurrah, throwing something, flowers, grain, up in the air in joy. She's saying, here, take it. Take these things and come join me.

So. I get down on my knees and search around under the bed for the suitcase. I pull it out, unzip it, open it up wide. The smell bolts out at me, so strong it's almost sickening. I reach in – soft, smooth, like her hair. I pull up her scarf they're right, a silk one – and bring it to my face. Just hanging in her wardrobe has made the whole thing smell forever and indelibly like her again, and already I feel reassured.

I wrap the scarf around my neck. The colour won't suit me, not like it suited her – purple, almost lavender – but, it will do.

Next, the underwear, which, oddly, doesn't smell like her, but like the soap in her drawer, spicy and clean. I smile. They were wrong. Not socks – who would want socks, as Doug rightly pointed out, in this weather. But they were on the right track. From the same drawer, but much better. I take my clothes off and slip into her underwear, squeeze myself into her bra. They are surprisingly sexy, not what I imagined her to have at all, cotton and useful, but silky, almost showy, in apricot satin with a thin line of cream lace.

And finally, the watch. One thing they haven't guessed, but then they wouldn't know that she removed it, put it on the side table out of force of nervous habit, that night. I slip it onto my wrist. It's lovely, understated, but heavy and expensive, stainless steel and 18 carat gold. Much nicer than mine, now adorning the wrist of a woman possibly in labour. Yes, I prefer this one, and am sorry I can't wear it all the time. Not yet anyway.

I move over to the mirror again. Dressed in her things, I can see more of her now, her height and stillness, especially in those last moments. And now I wonder – perhaps she had not given up, was not living in the past, away from herself. Perhaps there could have been a future, something between us. She never said no, after all, she never gave a clear indication.

I stare and stare at myself, at the rather pleasing compilation of the two of us I have become. In her things, like this, I have some of her frailty, I look like a smaller version of her, her little sister perhaps, the one she didn't have. And, like older sisters will, she merely found some things out first, and because I love her, I can forgive her. Besides, I'm not too far behind.

I run my hand across my stomach. Outside, I hear the crunch of gravel underfoot, presumably Doug leaving. Poor Doug. Back to a house both empty and full of Marilyn. He must know she's never coming back, that she's someplace else by now. And that because of who she is, her silence and reserve, her ordinary beauty, even her helplessness – because of all this, people will swarm to her like bees to honey. Somewhere else, she's not dead.

Adam comes up the stairs two at a time, silently past Aaron's bedroom. I hear him pause at ours, then he turns, almost as if following his nose, and at last appears behind me, framed in the doorway.

His eyes run over me, appreciatively I think. "Was that Doug?" I say, superfluously. He nods. "Yes. He – he doesn't want to see us again, he says. He wants to be alone."

"What about Lewis?" I say.

Guilt crosses Adam's face, and he shrugs.

"You forgot," I say. "Well, never mind. He'll be back. Men always are..."

Adam smiles, almost unwillingly. "What am I going to do with you," he says, then, out of the blue, "Did you sleep with her?"

I say the only thing I can say. "No." Then, "Did you?", although I already know the answer.

He sighs. "No. More's the pity." He glances at me.

We stare at each other through the mirror. He moves, and reaches round, rubs his thumbs lightly across my breasts, the smooth material. "These are hers then, I take it?"

"Yes."

He unwraps the scarf, and begins to move it, his hand covered by it, across my shoulders, along my back and stomach. "Like her hair," he says, reading my mind, "like her hair would feel falling over you."

I can hardly remain standing from desire, yet am also on the verge of tears. Adam drops the scarf and turns me around, reaches down to his trousers. I think, I need to lie down. But instead of lowering them, his hand reappears with a neatly folded tissue. He waves it in front of my face, then takes both hands off of me and unfolds it. There, right in the middle, is the perfect pink imprint of lips pressing away extra lipstick. I know at once they're Marilyn's.

He meets my eyes again. "I found it the night she left, in the bathroom. Folded up next to the sink, almost like she wanted someone to find it and take it. Like it was waiting to happen."

I don't know what to think. I am shaken to see that his eyes look heavy with something I can't identify, something I'm not accustomed to seeing there. Sorrow perhaps. Or resignation.

And yet, something must happen next. I reach for him. He tilts my head back, lays the tissue over my face. I hope he has placed it just right, so our lips are completely together. I inhale, and feel the tissue close inside my mouth.

He pauses. I wonder if Marilyn heard voices, like I think I do now. If someone was calling her home. I close my eyes, and feel the tissue lift slightly at the edges as Adam leans to kiss me.